X

SPACESHIP MEDIC

Spaceship Medic

BY HARRY HARRISON

Doubleday & Company, Inc., Garden City, New York
1970

Library of Congress Catalog Card Number 70–103750
Copyright © 1970 by Harry Harrison
All Rights Reserved
Printed in the United States of America
First Edition

SPACESHIP MEDIC

1

The run from the lunar station to Mars is a piece of cake. The passengers take the rocket buses up to the interplanetary spacer, the *Johannes Kepler,* and settle down for ninety-two days of fun and food, sociability and relaxation. All one hundred and forty-seven of the passengers were enjoying themselves, in just this way, on the thirtieth day out from Earth.

That was when the meteorite hit the spaceship head on. Almost dead center.

The automatic lasers did not stop it. The outer, armored hull barely slowed it down. It ripped its way through eighteen different compartments before burying itself deep in the cargo in the center of the drum-shaped ship.

On its destructive course it passed through the main control room, killing Captain Kardyd and twelve other officers and men. Sixteen passengers also died, in sudden exploding agony, and the main water tank was ruptured.

It was very bad indeed.

Lieutenant Donald Chase was stretched out on a bunk in

the sick bay when the meteorite hit, reading a thick book entitled *Bone Deterioration In Low-Gravity Environments*. The metal frame of his bunk vibrated, shaking the book, and for a few instants he ignored it.

Then the significance of what had happened struck him. Vibration! There are no shocks or sudden jars in a spaceship moving through a vacuum. He dropped the book and jumped to his feet just as all the alarms sounded at once.

A blaring horn hammered at his ears and the red emergency light blinked madly. An amplified recording thundered out, replacing the sound of the horn.

"SPACE EMERGENCY! THE HULL OF THIS SHIP HAS BEEN HOLED. THE SHIP IS LOSING AIR. THE AUTOMATIC DOORS ARE NOW CLOSING BETWEEN COMPARTMENTS. FOLLOW SPACE SURVIVAL DRILL."

At the moment the horn had been sounded, the emergency locker across the room had crashed open, activated by the same alarms that had sounded the warning.

"Strip and dress," Don called out, repeating the drill as he had been taught. At the time it had just been one more thing to learn. He had never thought that he might some day use it.

His one-piece shipsuit zipped open down the front, and he hopped along on one foot as he tore it off. He kicked off his lightweight sandals at the same time and jumped for the locker.

The emergency spacesuit was still rocking on the end of the arm that had snapped it out of the storage locker. It was a one-piece suit, almost skintight, cut to an exact fit for him. The helmet dangled forward, away from him, while the entire suit was open down the back.

"Head, right leg, left leg. Right arm, left arm, close," he mumbled to himself, repeating the drill.

Grabbing the handles on the supporting rack, Don bent forward and put his head into the helmet. At the same instant he kicked his right leg into the suit. Automatic valves blew compressed air into the leg so it puffed out like a balloon. As soon as his leg was all the way in, his toes tripped a switch and the air stopped. The suit leg collapsed firmly about his own.

Then the other leg and his arms, pushing in behind the expanding blast of air. He wriggled his fingers into the glove-like extensions of the arms and, as soon as they were all the way in, he reached out and punched the red knob with the white letters SEAL large upon it.

The closing device sat on the suit at the base of his spine. It began to suddenly wriggle upward, like a great insect, pulling the open edges of the suit together and sealing them. When it reached the helmet it dropped off and he was free. And his spacesuit was airtight.

The entire process, from beginning to end, had taken less than twelve seconds.

Don's helmet looked like a round fishbowl with a hole in front of his nose and mouth. A metal cover for this stood open, ready to snap shut if the air pressure fell below five pounds to the square inch. His suit contained only a limited supply of oxygen and this had to be saved until really needed.

The emergency medical kit was also in the open locker. He grabbed it up and ran over to the computer printout. This was an ordinary electric typewriter that was connected directly to the ship's computer. Don quickly typed out his code number. This identified him as the ship's medical officer so the computer would know how much information he was authorized to receive. Then he typed:

WHAT IS EMERGENCY?

There was less than a second's hesitation as the computer analyzed his question, found the desired information, checked to see if he was qualified to receive this type of information, then reached a decision. The typewriter sprang to life, the ball of the typing head flying across the paper.

HOLE IN OUTER HULL ABOVE COMPARTMENT 1∅7-JN
THIS COMPARTMENT AND 17 OTHERS IN AIRLESS CONDITION
AIRLESS COMPARTMENTS SEALED FROM REST OF SHIP
AIRLESS COMPARTMENTS ARE
1∅7-JN
32B
32BL

Don stepped to the chart of the ship and felt a sudden clutching in his chest as he saw that 1∅7-JN was the control room, the ship's brain.

As soon as the computer had finished tapping out the list of damage sites, he tore the sheet off and jammed it into the leg pocket of his suit. Grabbing up the medical kit, he ran out of the sick bay, heading toward control.

There were probably dead people in every one of the listed compartments. And perhaps some injured who might be saved if he worked fast enough. But only one compartment counted. The control room, and the men who worked there.

Without them this great spaceship would be just a spinning hunk of metal. It would tumble on through space, past Mars, and into the endless darkness.

Ahead was the stairwell that ran down from B deck to A deck, just outside the control room.

"What's happening? What's the alarm?" a frightened man in a purple suit said, coming out of a cabin and trying to block Don's way.

"Emergency. Stay in your cabin as you have been instructed."

Don brushed by him, sending him spinning aside when the man wouldn't move fast enough. He turned into the stairwell and collided with a closed door.

This was an automatic, airtight door, that had closed when the compartments had lost their air. Doors would have closed between every one of these compartments, as well as in the compartments on every side to prevent disaster from spreading.

A green light glowed on the panel in the frame: the compartment beyond had air in it. Don was trying to fumble the override key from his leg pocket when running footsteps sounded behind him.

"Let me open it, Doc," the man called out. Don stood aside.

It was a crewman, Electrician's Mate Gold, who was also wearing a spacesuit with open helmet. All of the crew members—the surviving crew members—would have them on by now. Gold slipped his key into the lock and the door slid open, closing solidly behind them as soon as they were through. They went down the stairs two at a time.

The door at the foot was closed and a red light glowed beside it.

"They've run out of air," Gold said, his voice suddenly hollow.

"We'll have to get in there."

"Better use your key, Doc. Mine won't override to an evacuated compartment."

Air, the breath of life, could not be spared in a spaceship moving between the planets. Only a few officers had keys that would open the doors when there was a vacuum on the other side. Don put in his key and turned.

They could hear the laboring electric motors that fought to overcome the pressure: then the door began to slide slowly sideways. As soon as a hairline crack opened a monster hissing began. It grew louder as the crack widened, and their eardrums popped as the air was expelled from the stairwell.

There was a sudden *clack, clack,* barely heard in the rarefied atmosphere, as the coverplates in front of their helmets snapped shut automatically.

The door opened wide and they stepped through.

They were in the section of corridor just before the control room. The airtight doors at each end were closed, making a sealed compartment. Across from them they could see the control room door, partly open.

It was held from closing by Captain Kardyd's body.

The captain's eyes were open, blue and empty and frozen, staring at them. There was a fixed expression of anger on his face, as though he were annoyed at them for not reaching him in time. Don looked away from those accusing eyes and turned his key in the lock. The door slid open and they stepped inside, their feet soundlessly slapping the metal decking in the vacuum.

The events of the tragedy could be read with terrible clarity from the huddle of bodies by the door. The men nearest the exit had tried to reach it when the accident had occurred. Yet, even as they had battled for their own lives, the officers and men had seen to it that the captain went first. He was the most important man aboard. Two of the men had their fingers still curled where they had grabbed the door and tried to stop it from closing on him. The first mate's key was in his fingers. He had tried to insert it into the override lock.

They had all failed.

They had all died.

As had everyone else in the room. The bodies were heaped in frozen profusion, curled in final agonies. Don went and looked down at the ruin of the communicator station. The large radio was wrecked and twisted, and flying gobbets of molten metal had splattered in all directions. When he bent over he could see down through the hole, as big as fist, that penetrated the insulation, the water chamber, and the hull. Stars moved by in the darkness at the other end. Turning, he looked at the hole the meteorite had made in the opposite bulkhead as it tore on in its path of destruction. There was nothing he could do here with the dead. He would have to care for the living. As he turned to go he saw Electrician's Mate Gold waving to him. They walked close and touched helmets.

"Can you get a patch on that hole?" Don asked, his voice carried by the vibration of helmet to helmet.

"Sure, that's easy enough, Doc. There are temporaries here that will work until the hull gang get outside and make repairs. But that's not what is important."

"What do you mean?"

"Look at all these bodies. Too many. There shouldn't be this many guys in control at the same time. And look at all the gold braid."

Working swiftly, numbed by the same fear, they turned over the dead men and looked at their faces. When they touched helmets again it was Don who spoke for both of them.

"The captain must have been having a meeting of his officers. They're all here, every one of them."

Gold nodded in solemn agreement, his helmet sliding across the other as he moved his head.

"Every deck officer," he said. "And even the second engineer. Which means you better cross your fingers, Doc, that we find First Engineer Holtz. And that he is in the green."

"You can't mean . . ."

"It's true, Doc. If the first engineer is dead, or even hurt, you are the only officer left aboard.

"You'll be in charge of this ship."

2

There was nothing for a doctor to do in the control room. A Damage Control party was pushing their way in and, as soon as they had cleared the doorway, Don made his way back to the pressurized section of the ship. A temporary airlock had been fastened to the door at the top of the stairwell and he cycled through it. As the pressure hit the valve on his chest the metal cover in the front of his helmet popped open and he was breathing the ship's atmosphere again. He went to the nearest viewer, checked the directory posted beside it, then dialed for Damage Control. The line was engaged, but the flashing green light indicated that his call was being held and he would be connected as soon as possible.

Don shifted his weight impatiently from leg to leg. This was not quite the kind of a voyage he had expected. There was supposed to be very little glamor or adventure in the space service these days. Many young doctors, fresh out of medical school as he was, served a hitch on the spacers while they made up their minds as to their future. There were many good positions opened for doctors on the satellite stations and the planetary bases. This was a good way to look at them before coming to a decision. It was also a pleasant change after the years of medical school. Pleasant! He had to smile at his reflected image in the phone screen—just as the call signal chimed.

"Dr. Chase here," he said to the harried petty officer who swam into focus on the small screen.

"Got some business for you, Doc. Worse one of them seems to be lying outside of compartment 32B. If you go there I'll have the information on the others waiting for you."

"Positive. Out."

He ran. In accidents minutes, even seconds, can mean the difference between life and death.

A gray-haired man was lying in the corridor in front of 32B and a young girl was bending over him. She was wearing a yellow playsuit—with only one sleeve. When she moved aside he saw that she had torn it off and wadded it up to make a bandage for the side of the man's face. It was stained red with blood.

"I didn't move him or anything, Doctor, just tried to stop the bleeding. That's all."

"You did fine," he said, kneeling and snapping open his case.

The first thing he did was push the recording telltale against the man's flaccid wrist. The bands slipped out and automatically clamped the instrument into place. The dials quivered to life and Don saw that the patient's blood pressure was low, his pulse weak, his temperature normal, his skin cold and clammy. Shock. That was only to be expected. Before looking at the wound, he slipped out a spray hypodermic that shot the antishock drug through the man's skin without making a puncture. When he did lift off the makeshift bandage he saw that it was far less serious than the girl had imagined. The wound was superficial, just a jagged tear in the skin. But there was so much bleeding that it had looked bad to her untrained eye. He sprayed the wound with derma-foam. It would stiffen and prevent further bleeding until he could treat the patient in the operating room.

"He'll be all right," Don said. "Were you with him when it happened? Are you injured yourself?"

"No, I'm fine. I just came down the corridor and found him like this. Just lying there in the pool of blood. After I put the bandage on and made the call for help I noticed that thing in the wall. But I have no idea how it got there."

She pointed to a jagged chunk of metal that was embedded in the corridor wall opposite compartment 32B. The red light was on next to the sealed door.

"It was just bad luck," Don said. "There was an explosion in that compartment just as he was passing and that piece of metal must have come through the door and hit him." He did not add that the metal was from the passage of the meteorite and that the compartment was now airless. The metal must have exploded out through the doorway before it automatically closed.

Announcement chimes sounded from the speaker in the corridor, and would be heard at the same time in every compartment in the great ship. There was a pause, then someone coughed and began speaking.

"Attention, please. This is First Engineer Holtz speaking. I have been asked to inform everyone aboard, passengers and crew, that this spacer has had an accident. We have been struck by a meteorite."

The girl gasped with shock and raised her hands before her face.

"It's all right," Don said quickly. "There is no danger. A few compartments were holed, but they are already sealed off." He thought to himself that Holtz might be a good engineer, but he knew nothing at all about people to make a frightening statement like this one. The amplified voice continued.

"I am informed by Damage Control that the holed compartments have been sealed off and repairs are being made. Passengers are ordered to remain in their cabins or wherever they are now, and should not move about. The crewmen are doing their work and you will only interfere with them. That is all."

A spacesuited man with a folding stretcher came hurrying up.

"Damage Control sent me, Doc," he said. "Gave me a message for you."

He dug the folded slip of paper out of his leg pocket and handed it to Don. It was computer printout that listed the location of all the wounded that had been reported so far. Don looked for the nearest one.

"This man will have to go to the sick bay," he said. "But you'll need someone else on the other end of that stretcher. . . ."

"I can help," the girl said.

Don made a quick decision. She was young and strong and should be able to carry her weight.

"All right," he said. "You can stay with the patient in the sick bay."

"What about me, Doc?" the crewman asked.

"Bring the stretcher back with you. I'll be near compartment 89-HA. Try and pick up someone else for the other end on your way."

The man at compartment 89-HA was dead. As were the next two people on the list, passengers, an elderly couple. Cold vacuum is a killer that spares very few. But there were survivors, people who had been in the compartments that had been the last to be holed, from which the air had been expelled a little more slowly. Don treated them for shock, burst blood vessels, and minor wounds. There were pitifully few of them in comparison to the number of dead. He was bandaging a frostbitten hand when the announcement sounded from the speaker.

"Lieutenant Chase, will you report to the control room. Officers meeting."

A *very* small meeting, Don thought grimly. He looked around at the few patients in the sick bay, all sedated, mostly asleep. A young crewman was rolling up the stretcher for storage and Don called him over.

"Rama, do you think you can keep an eye on things while I go up to control?"

"In the green, Doctor. I'll call if there is any trouble."

Rama Kusum was an engine room mate—but his ambition was to be a doctor some day. He saved most of his salary so he could go to medical school at home in India. In his off duty hours he had been helping Don and learning what he could.

Damage Control had called through earlier that the hull seals were in place, so that spacesuits could now be removed. Don had not had the time to do anything about it. Now he gratefully peeled off the hot suit and quickly washed before putting on a clean shipsuit.

He retraced his earlier route to the control room. Only now all the doors were open. As he went down the stairs to A deck he found the railing was cold to his touch, and that the metal walls were damp where moisture was condensing out of the air. They would warm up quickly enough and the water would evaporate.

The bodies were gone from the control room and a heavy metal plate had been welded over the raw hole in the floor where the meteorite had crashed through. Someone had been at work on the ruined radio and its parts were spread across the deck. At first Don thought he was alone, until he heard the cough and saw someone was sitting in the astrogator's high-backed chair. It was First Engineer Holtz.

"Come in and close that door," Holtz said when he looked up and saw Don. "And sit down, Lieutenant, we have a lot here to talk about. A very lot." He waved the handful of papers he held, and looked unhappy.

Don dropped into a chair and waited for the other man to begin. It was a long wait. Holtz brooded over the papers, flipping through them slowly, as though there was an answer hidden there that he had missed. He was not a young man, and he seemed even older after the shocking events of the past few hours. The skin hung in dark bags under his eyes and sagged loosely under his chin.

"Things look very bad," he finally said.

"What exactly do you mean?" Don asked, controlling his impatience. Holtz was the senior officer and therefore automatically in command of the ship.

"Just look at these!" he shook the papers angrily. "Every officer dead except you and me. How could that have happened? And this flying piece of rock has destroyed our radio, the big one we must have. Sparks is making a jury rig, but the power will be limited. Not that it makes much difference. There are no ships in any orbit that could possibly help us. And almost half our water is gone, thrown when that hole was made. Terrible!"

Don felt he had to do something to interrupt the tale of woe.

"It's bad, sir, but it's not the end of the ship. The death of the captain, and the others, is a tragedy, but we are just going to have to learn to live with it. We can get the ship through. We're on course and in orbit, and when we get closer to Mars we'll make contact and navigating officers can come out to meet us. The ship is sealed and sound. We'll make it. You can count upon me for any help I can offer." He smiled. "It will work out, Captain."

"Captain!" Holtz sat up, his eyes widening.

"Of course. You're the senior officer and the rank passes automatically to you. . . ."

"No it doesn't!" He shook his head fiercely. "I am the first engineer. The atomic pile and the engines are my duty. I know nothing about astrogation, nothing. I cannot leave the power room, I'm sorry. You want someone to call captain, then call yourself captain."

"But—I'm just a doctor," Don protested. "This is my first space trip. You have to—"

"Don't tell me what I have to do. *I* tell *you*. I must be in the power room, there is no way to get around that. You are in charge, the captain until other officers come aboard. The ratings know their jobs, they'll help you." Holtz's anger collapsed suddenly, and when he clasped his big hands together before him Don could see that they were shaking.

"You're a young man," Holtz explained. "You'll find a way to do the job. I can't. I'm going to retire, you know about that, this was supposed to be my last trip. I know atomics and I know engines. I know where I belong." He straightened and looked Don in the eye. "That is the way it has to be. You're in charge."

Don started to protest just as the door opened to the passageway. Computerman Boyd came in. He saluted quickly in the direction of the captain's chair, then turned to the two officers.

"I have the readings here on the observations," he said, but Holtz interrupted him.

"You will make your report to Lieutenant Chase. I must return to the power room. We have reached agreement that he is to be in charge until other officers come aboard. Make your report to him."

Holtz got up as he finished speaking and stamped out. There was nothing that Don could say. The chief engineer could not be forced to take on the captain's responsibilities. There was no way out of this. The computerman turned to Don and handed him a sheet of paper.

"Here are the course corrections worked out from the hourly observations, Doc. The first ones since the rock hit."

Don looked blankly at the rows of numbers on the paper. "What does all this mean? You're going to have to do some translation for me, Boyd."

"I don't know much about this myself, Doc, but I used to work with the astrogator. He was talking about making a course correction during the next watch, but now I don't know. That rock hit right on the plane of rotation and it had enough mass and speed to affect us. Didn't slow the rotation enough to feel, we still have about one G on us, but it knocked us a bit off center and the ship is starting to precess."

Don sighed and handed the paper back. "You're going to have to make it a lot simpler than that, Boyd, if you want me to make head or tail of the problem."

The computerman was not smiling. "Well—our main axis, the thrust of our atomic jets is aimed ahead on our course. At least it used to be, and it *has* to be for any course corrections. But now we're beginning to tumble, you know, sort of turn end over end. While the ship is doing that we can't make any course corrections. And, Doc, unless we make those corrections we're going to miss Mars and keep right on going. Forever."

Don nodded. He could understand that. Something had to be done—and fast—and he was the only one who could do it. Holtz wasn't going to help and there was no one else aboard the *Johannes Kepler* whom he could turn to.

"All right, Boyd," he said, "I'll take care of this. But if I do, you are going to have to stop calling me 'Doc.'"

"Yes, sir," the computerman said, straightening up and saluting. "I understand, Captain."

3

"You sent for me, sir?"

Don looked up and saw Chief Petty Officer Kurikka at the entrance to the wardroom. He waved him forward.

"Come in, Chief. I'm having a meeting in about a half an hour, but I wanted to talk to you first. If anyone is able to answer my questions about the *Johannes Kepler*, you should be the one." He pointed to the model of the spacer on the table before him. "I understand that you have been aboard this ship since she was commissioned?"

"Longer than that, sir. I was in the construction gang that assembled the Big Joe in Earth orbit. I switched to the space service then and stayed aboard her."

With his fair hair and blue eyes the tall Finn did not show his years at all.

"Better than I thought," Don said. "Do you think you could explain to me about the precession and wobble that has the computermen so worried?"

Kurikka nodded, and carefully unfastened the model of the ship from its base and held it before him.

"The way they described the Big Joe to us when we were building her is the best way I know. It's a bass drum hooked to a basketball by a gas pipe."

"You're right—once you hear that you can't forget it."

"The gas pipe passes through the heads of the drum, with a little sticking out on one side, and all the rest of it on the other. The basketball is on the end of the long chunk of pipe. In the ball is the atomic reactor and the engines. Where the ball is hooked to the pipe is all the radiation insulation and the engine room. Everything else in the ship is in the drum. When we are in orbit the whole ship rotates around the main axis of the pipe—which is called the midpipe."

"I'm with you so far," Don said, and tapped the drum with his finger. "And the drum rotates fast enough so that the centrifugal force generates the equivalent of one gravity here on A deck. A deck is the first deck in and, like all the decks, goes all the way around the drum. The floor under our feet is the outside skin of the ship. We go up one flight, 'up' really being in toward the center of rotation, to B deck. Then to C deck, which is cargo and storage only, and the last pressurized deck. The interior of the drum is open to space and is for cargo only. Am I right so far?"

"In the green, sir." Kurikka's impassive face almost bent into a smile, but not quite.

Don spun the pipe between his hands so that the model rotated, and, at the same time, aimed the drum at the light above the table.

"So here is the ship in flight, spinning as she goes. And aiming at that light which we'll call Mars."

"That's not *quite* right, sir. After takeoff and flameout the ship was flipped end for end, so our main jets are now pointed at Mars. The observatory, back here where the stub of pipe sticks through the drum, is pointed back the way we came."

Don turned the model end for end and examined it. "So this is the way we are moving—and spinning at the same time. Then what is wrong?"

The chief pointed. "The axis of rotation of our midpipe should be right on line with our course. In that way jets fore or aft can speed us up or slow us down in orbit. We get to the same spot, but we get there sooner or later. Or if course change is needed the lateral jets, here on the center of balance on the midpipe, can alter our course sideways in any degree that is needed. None of that is possible now."

"Why?"

"Because the meteorite started the axis of our rotation shifting. We're no longer pointing straight down the orbit, and the change is continuing. It's a mighty slow tumble, but that's just what it is. We're tumbling along through space. We can't make any course corrections until we can straighten out the tumble."

"And unless we do make the course corrections we're going to miss Mars completely."

With slow seriousness, Chief Kurikka nodded agreement. The long silence that followed was broken by a brisk rapping on the wardroom door. The chief went over and opened it. Computerman Boyd was outside.

"0300 hours, Captain," he said. "The purser is here with me and Commander Holtz said to tell you he'll be along shortly."

"Come in then. We can get started without him."

They entered the wardroom—followed by a man whom Don had never seen before. He had straight black hair, now graying, a great flowing mustache, and coppery skin. One of the passengers—but what was he doing here? Before Don could ask the obvious question the purser, Jonquet, stepped forward. He was Swiss, and he had been trained as a hotel manager. So that, even after years in space, he still carried the feeling of a grand hotel about him. He made what could only have been a slight bow and indicated the man with him.

"I hope you will excuse me, Captain, but I have taken the liberty of bringing someone to this assembly whom I wish you to meet. This is Dr. Ugalde, of the University of Mexico. He is one of the foremost mathematicians in the world. I thought that," his voice lowered, "with the death of the other officers, Dr. Ugalde might be able to supply us with aid of importance."

Don could not be angry. Of course the purser had no business making decisions without asking him first. But he, a doctor of medicine, had no business acting like a captain. The two canceled out.

"Thank you," Don said. "It was a good idea that I should have thought of myself. Since mathematics seem to be at the core of our problem."

"Do not expect too much!" Ugalde said, waving his hands excitedly. "Between the airy heights of abstract mathematics and the practicalities of flying a spaceship is a universe of difference. I have no experience. . . ."

"None of us has the experience we need," Don broke in. "We are going to have to feel our way along, so we can certainly use your help, Doctor. I ask only that you do not reveal to the other passengers how many officers have been killed and what a plight we are in."

"My word of honor!" Ugalde said, standing up straight and placing his hand over his heart. "My noble ancestors fought for the freedom of my country and many of them died in its cause. I can do no less."

Don could not quite see the connection between this and their present danger, but he nodded agreement nevertheless, and asked them all to be seated. Then he explained their problem and the difficulty of correcting it without the skilled knowledge of the dead officers.

"That's the picture," he concluded, "and it's not good. Boyd, what's the usual drill in a course correction?"

The computerman chewed his lip and looked around nervously.

"I can't really say, sir. The astrogator would give me the figures already processed for the computer, and I wouldn't do much more than check for transcription errors and feed them into the machine. Sometimes, on complex problems, we would send the figures to Mars Central. They have bigger computers there and staff mathematicians." His eyes widened at a sudden idea. "Say, couldn't we do that. Get help by radio, I mean?"

Don shook his head sadly.

"We can't do that—and I don't want that information to leave this room. The main transceiver has been knocked out. The radio operator is jury-rigging a transmitter and receiver. But we don't know how long it will take him—or how powerful they will be when he is finished. So, at least for the moment, we have to forget about outside aid." He turned to the mathematician. "Can you help us with this problem?" he asked.

Dr. Ugalde stood up instantly and began to pace the floor, one hand behind his back. He seemed to think better this way. "Impossible, impossible," he said. "Astrogation as an applied science is a world removed from theoretical mathematics. I know nothing of the forces and measurements involved. A three body problem, of course, that is not difficult. But . . ."

"But do you think you could talk to Computerman Boyd and look at the log for the previous readings and course corrections, and possibly come up with an answer?"

"I can try, that is all I can promise. I will try."

"Good. Please report to me what your conclusions are." Don looked at a list he had scrawled out. "We have another problem facing us. We lost a good deal of water when the hull was cracked. . . ."

"We shall die of thirst!" Dr. Ugalde said, on his feet again, thinking perhaps of the parching deserts of Mexico.

Don had to smile when he answered. "Not, really, Doctor. That's not our problem. The ship is a closed system and all the water is recycled. But this is water that serves other functions. It circulates between the double outer skin of the ship and acts as a radiation barrier, shielding us from the Van Allen radiation when leaving Earth, and solar radiation the rest of the time. Right now is the time of a quiet sun, so I don't think we have to worry about radiation. However, we still have to breathe. The water is an essential part of the air purification of the Big Joe. Single-celled plants live in the water, and are pumped past transparent panels in the outer skin. They remove the carbon dioxide that we are breathing out all the time, and convert it to oxygen—that we need for life. A good number of these plants are gone, and they do not increase their numbers swiftly."

"What can we do about this?" the purser asked.

"We can't stop breathing," Don told him. "But we can stop free combustion that uses up oxygen. I notice that a number of passengers and crewmen smoke. The habit seems to be getting popular again now that cancer-free tobacco has been perfected. I want all the cigarettes, pipes, matches, everything like that confiscated and brought to me. Can you take care of this?"

The purser nodded. "I'll need at least two crewmen to help me, but I can take care of it."

"Good. I leave it up to you, then." Don looked at his list, and frowned. "The next item is a sad but necessary one. The bodies of the dead passengers, officers, and crewmen have been placed in the unpressurized hold to be brought to Mars. However I have found Captain Kardyd's will in his safe. It says—in very positive language—that he wishes immediate burial in space. If possible from his own ship. I think this leaves us no alternative. Does anyone here know anything about this ceremony?"

"I do, sir," Chief Kurikka said. "If you would let me, I would like to take care of this myself. I served under the captain for nine years."

Before Don could answer him the phone on the table rang. He nodded agreement to the chief and picked up the handset.

"Captain here," he said, a little ashamed to use the title in front of the others, although no one made any protest. He listened to the brief message and hung up with a single word of agreement.

"This is of importance to all of you," he said quietly. "That was the radio operator. He has assembled a receiver and has managed to pick up Mars Central. The signal is very weak and almost lost in static, but he is recording it and trying to make some sense out of it. He said that the same signal is being repeated over and over. Our call sign, he recognized that, and a very brief message. So far he can't make out most of it, but he has worked out part of it.

"They repeat *danger* over and over again. And the code word *sunspot.* . . ."

"That is no code word," First Engineer Holtz said from the doorway. "That is what I have come to tell you. I've detected it on my hull instruments. There is a solar storm coming." He paused and sighed, shudderingly, before he could finish speaking.

"A solar storm. That means we are all good as dead right now!"

4

"There is no cause to panic—and we cannot afford to even get excited," Don shouted over the voices and loud questions. "I want absolute silence in here!"

It worked. The trained spacemen were used to taking orders, so they obeyed the command. Dr. Ugalde was just as quiet as the rest. Don was standing, and he remained standing as he swept his glance over the others, almost forcing them back into their chairs with the intensity of his gaze. Holtz was still standing in the doorway and, as he opened his mouth to speak again, Don stabbed an angry finger at him.

"First Engineer Holtz. You will close that door and be seated. Then you will give your report in a proper manner. Without being too defeatist, if you can possibly manage that."

Don was not intentionally cruel to the older man. But he could not allow Holtz's panic to spread. The engineer flushed red and started to say something. Don would not hear him.

"I said sit down first. That order was very clear." Don was angry now and it could be heard in his voice.

Holtz wavered for a moment, then his shoulders slumped.

He closed the door and dropped loosely into the nearest chair. When he spoke his voice was hollow with defeat.

"Why fight. This was going to be my last voyage, now it is the last voyage for all of us. . . ."

"What do your instruments read?" Don broke in.

The first engineer's head hung down as he spoke, and his voice was so low that they had to strain to make out his words.

"Solar radiation . . . going up, going up steadily. I know what that is. Sunspots, a solar storm, and no way to guard against it."

"What does he mean?" the purser asked. "We've ridden out solar storms before without any trouble. Why should one bother us now?"

"Could I answer that?" Chief Kurikka asked. Don nodded to him.

"We've lost too much water, that's our main trouble. The water in the ship's double skin absorbs most of the charged particles sent out by the solar storm, slowing and stopping them. Just like the atmosphere on Earth. With half our water gone there isn't enough thickness to stop the radiation. And if Mars Central is sending out a warning, this storm must be worse than most. It's going to be a tough one to lick."

"But we're *going* to lick it," Don broke in. "Have there been any special precautions taken in the past for strong storms?"

"Yes, sir. We shift axis to point the reactor ball at the sun. This puts the mass of the reactor between the engine room and the sun, so the passengers are protected. Then all of the water is pumped into the emergency space on the head of the drum in that direction. As long as the ship keeps the correct orientation there is enough protection."

"Do we have enough water left for that trick?" Don asked.

The chief petty officer's expression did not change as he answered.

"No, sir, we do not."

"But the engine room will still be protected?"

"That is correct."

Don smiled. "Then that is half our problem. Passengers and crew to the engine room for the duration of the emergency. Take care of that, Purser." The first engineer started to protest about the space, but Don waved him to silence.

"Crowding won't hurt us, but radiation will kill us. We'll find room for everyone. But first we have to find a way to shift our axis. We will have to work as fast as possible because we don't know how much time we have. Yes, Boyd."

"I think I can be of some help there," the computerman said. "We have had garbled radio messages before during solar flares, and the computer is set up to process them. Multiple recordings are made, since the same message is sent over and over again, and run through the computer. The machine picks out the meaningful parts and assembles them for a complete message."

"That sounds good," Don told him. "Get cracking now on those recordings."

"Yes, sir," Boyd said, trying not to run until he had got through the door.

They all had important work to do and, one by one, they received their instructions and left. Only when they had gone did Don realize that he had nothing to do with the ship's problems until they came up with some answers. His medical tasks were done for the moment. He had treated all of the injuries, and the two serious cases were in the sick bay and under sedation. They were both attached to telltales that made continuous readings of their blood pressure, temperature, respiration, heartbeat, brain waves, and all the other factors that had to be watched. If any of these changed he would be warned at the same moment by the alarm on his belt.

For a few moments no one was bothering him and he could be alone. Sleep was out of the question. There would be plenty of time for that later if they avoided the present trouble. Even while he was thinking about this, his feet were making up his mind for him. Without consciously coming to a decision, he was out in the corridor and heading for the nearby elevator. The observatory, of course, that was where he wanted to go. While the elevator crawled up its shaft he called the duty man in the control room and reported where he would be.

The elevator went up from the outer skin, really inward to the midpipe that connected the two sections of the spacecraft. When the elevator stopped and the door slid open, Don grabbed the edges and pulled himself forward. With gentle ease he floated out, hanging suspended in midair. As soon as he touched the far side of the padded midpipe he grabbed one of the flexible handles located there and pulled himself toward the observatory.

Since the spaceship, with its engines turned off, was in free fall, there was no feeling of weight or gravity at all. The rotation of the ship created centrifugal force in the outer deck areas. But here, at the center of rotation, the forces were canceled out and he could float as easily as a fish in water. The observatory door opened when he touched the button and he drifted through.

As always, the breath caught in his throat at the incredible sight. Stars, rivers of stars, galaxies of them turning slowly before his eyes.

The observatory was a great transparent bowl at the end of

the midpipe, where it projected from the drum. Here, without any air in the way to diffract and dim them, the stars did not twinkle. They were hot points of light, of different colors and varying brightness, filling the bowl of darkness overhead. It was easy to forget the transparent covering and feel the sensation of being with them, among them, a part of the infinity of the universe.

There was the sun, off to one side, its glare automatically dimmed by the material of the dome. It reminded Don of the storm, already brewing on that fiery surface, and he checked the radiation counter. It was up slightly, but not enough to cause damage. Going up steadily, that's what Holtz had said. How much time did they have before that storm of destroying particles hit? And what could he possibly do to save the lives of all the people in his care? He pressed his clenched fists to the cool surface of the dome.

If there was a time for despair, this was it, when he was alone and unseen. He was tired, almost exhausted, and part of him wanted to give up on the spot. Pass the buck to someone else. There, in the darkness, he smiled at the thought. There was no one else: this was where the buck stopped. As a doctor he had been trained to accept responsibility for life and death. He had never thought when he took his Hippocratic oath that it would include being captain of a spaceship. He hadn't learned much about *that* in medical school! He smiled again at this thought and felt better. He would keep doing the job, to the best of his ability. That was the only source open to him.

The phone buzzed, loud in the silence of the galaxy-embracing chamber. He picked it up.

"Captain here," he said automatically, now that the decision had been made.

"Control room, sir. The tapes of the message from Mars Central have been processed by the computer. I have a transcription here of the complete message—do you want to hear it?"

"Just the figures. How strong is the storm going to be—and when does it hit us?"

"Just a moment . . . here it is. Force eight on the Hoyle scale. Ten is the tops, and I've never seen one over six before. . . ."

"So it's strong. I get the message. Now, when is it due."

"One and a half hours at the soonest. May be delayed a few minutes past that, but no more."

Don silently expelled the breath that he had, unknowingly, been holding. "All right. I'm on my way to control. Contact a passenger named Ugalde and have him meet me there soonest. And Chief Kurikka as well."

Ninety minutes to turn the ship. It didn't seem possible. But it *had* to be done. Concentrating fiercely, Don found his way automatically back to the control room, to face a furious Dr. Ugalde.

"The impossible you ask of me, Captain, and then to do it immediately. And *then* you interrupt! Such things cannot be. . . ."

"Less than an hour and a half until the storm arrives," Don said quietly. "Our time has run out, Doctor."

Ugalde's face went gray and he half dropped into the chair next to him. "Then . . . it is all too late," he whispered.

"I don't think so. We are just going to have to make the maneuvers by the seat of our pants." Don had to smile when he saw the shocked expressions on the faces of Kurikka and the duty man. "We have no other choice—and I wish you wouldn't look so astonished. You all know that commercial jetliners are almost completely controlled by automatic devices. Yet I'll bet you all have flown your own light planes or copters yourself. Spacers are no different. The first astronauts had to fly by wire when the automatics went out. We'll do the same. Kurikka, just what is involved in an attitude change, to move the axis of rotation?"

The chief looked gloomier than ever. "It's all done by the computer, sir. The astrogator feeds in the data and instructions, then we just sit back and watch it happen."

"Isn't there a provision for manual control, in case something should go wrong?"

"There is, though we have never had to use it. Those controls there."

Don went over to the indicated board and looked at the dials and switches. "Now can you—simply—tell me what happens when an attitude change is made?"

None of this was by the book, and Chief Kurikka lived by the book. Yet he was intelligent enough to know that there were times when the book had to be thrown away. Reluctantly, in spite of himself, he came to the control board and switched on the screens.

"There are two television pickups," he said. "One in the bow, in the observatory, and the other in the stern. It's on the centerline between the main drive rockets. This is the bow picture."

He pointed to the screen with the sun appearing off to one side, the same scene that Don had watched from the observatory. Kurikka continued.

"There is a track around the reactor sphere, just at the base of the main tubes. A small reaction rocket rides this track, moving in the direction opposite to our spin. This cancels out the spin so that the rocket always faces the same direction. A short burst is fired, just enough to start the ship tumbling, end over end. The ship turns until it is orientated in the new direction—then the computer fires the rocket again canceling out the motion."

Don looked at his watch, then forced himself to look away without seeing how little time was left. There was a simple answer here. Almost too simple, he realized. He turned and motioned to the Mexican mathematician.

"Dr. Ugalde—would you come here please and check me out. You've heard what the chief said, so you know our problem. The sun is now before our bow, just about 180 degrees wrong. Now, if the rocket were fired the ship would turn end for end in space. When the sun appeared in the middle of this stern screen we would be facing in the right direction, with the reactor between us and the solar storm. At that time the jet will be facing in the opposite direction, and if it were fired the rotation would stop and our attitude would be correct. Will that work?"

Ugalde frowned in concentration, then scribbled some brief equations in his leather-bound note pad.

"It won't work that easily," he said. "The second rocket blast must be exactly as long as the first, and must be timed so that it ends with the ship on the correct orientation. . . ."

"Not the details, Doctor, please. Just tell us if it will work or not."

The mathematician looked surprised. "Of course it will work! Why shouldn't it? It is just what the computer does. You will be doing the same thing, only much more crudely."

"Crude or not, it's going to save our lives!" Don smacked his fist into his palm excitedly. "Start now, if you please. With your theory and Chief Kurikka's knowledge of the controls you should be able to do the job between you."

Now he permitted himself to look at his watch and he almost gasped aloud at how little time there was left. Less than forty-five minutes remained before the solar storm of deadly radiation would hit.

"Purser Jonquet on the phone for you, Captain," a voice said, breaking into his thoughts. The duty man was holding the phone out to him.

"Captain here."

"This is the purser, Captain. There seems to be a little trouble with the passengers. I wonder if I could ask you to come here and talk to them."

"Not now. There is no time. I'll join you there in the engine room as soon as I can, and talk to them then."

There was a moment's pause before the purser spoke again. This time there was more than a little concern in his voice.

"That's what I want you to talk to them about, sir. They're not in the engine room. All of them have had a meeting, here in the main dining hall, and they say they aren't moving until they talk to the captain or a senior officer."

"But—don't they know that they are all dead?"

The purser's voice was softer, as if he were whispering into the telephone so that no one would hear.

"No, sir, not quite. I did not want to alarm them so I deliberately kept the details vague as to the immediacy of the emergency. Could you come here and explain to them?"

Don thought swiftly—could he? He realized now that he had made a mistake in forgetting about the passengers. Treating them like cargo, or sheep to be herded around. Everything should have been explained to them earlier. Now he would have to tell them the truth. Quickly. There were only minutes remaining.

"I'll be right down," he said, and hung up the phone.

"Captain, this is most important," Dr. Ugalde called out as he saw Don rise.

"What is it?" Don asked, walking over to join them at the controls. The sun wobbled slowly off the stern screen while he watched.

"Here, see for yourself," Ugalde said. "In theory it is fine to say we turn the ship by eye and hand. In practice it is something different. It can be done, and we are getting close. But we cannot make as precise an adjustment as the computer, with a ship of the great mass of this one. The sun will be aligned correctly, but will drift slowly off. Someone must make corrections constantly until all the drift has been eliminated and we are orientated correctly."

"Do you have any idea of how long this will take?" Don asked, hoping, but knowing in advance what the answer will be.

"Hours, surely. It is most delicate work."

"Hours! That means whoever stays here at the controls will be unprotected from the storm and will be exposed to certain death."

"I realize that. . . . Someone must die to save the others. Is that not a good way for a man to die?"

Don looked at his watch through a growing haze of desperation. Just a little over a half an hour left. It couldn't be done, there wasn't enough time for anything.

The crew and passengers, they were all as good as dead.

5

"One shall die so that all shall live," Ugalde said, squaring his shoulders and stepping forward. "It will be my pleasure to control the ship. Everyone else must go instantly to the engine room."

The little doctor might have looked funny, with his chin up and his hand laid across his heart, but he did not. He meant what he had said, and would not hesitate to die for this shipload of strangers.

"I don't think that will be necessary, Doctor," Don told him. "We'll find a way out of this without sacrificing any lives."

"May I inquire how that is to be done, Captain?"

How indeed! Don thought—and felt a moment of silent panic. How could this be done? There had to be a way. The crew knew the ship better than he did. He had to force them to think.

"What about a radiation suit, Chief?" Don asked. "I know we have them. Couldn't the man who was piloting wear one?"

Kurikka's face was pure Scandinavian gloom as he shook his head *no*.

"Not a chance. The ones we have aboard are for limited use at low radiation levels. Just about as good as tissue paper in the storm that's coming."

Don refused to give in to the over-all feeling of despair.

"There must be a way. Can't duplicate controls be rigged in the engine room, something like that?"

"Possibly, given enough time, we'd have to string cables. . . ."

"Something else then, if there isn't time for that." Don looked around, searching for inspiration. That door, in the wall, leading to the small service washroom. He pulled it open.

"What about this? Rig cables in here, it's only a few feet. We could put in something to stop the radiation, lead sheets. . . ."

And then, just that suddenly, it was all clear. He knew what had to be done. He turned, pointing at the chief, thinking aloud.

"A spacesuit. It keeps air in—so it should keep water out. Am I right?"

Kurikka rubbed his jaw. "Well, I guess it could. But the water wouldn't do the suit any good. Rust and—"

"That won't happen in a couple of hours," Don snapped, aware of the seconds rushing by. "Here's what you must do. Rig a set of controls inside this washroom and connect them up. Put in a repeater screen. If the door isn't waterproof get some patching gunk and seal it. Get a spacesuit and make sure that oxygen tanks are full." He started toward the door. "The pilot will work from the washroom—which will be filled with water."

"But, sir," Kurikka called after him. "How can we water-proof the controls . . . ?"

"Find a way. Put them in plastic bags for all I care. But do it"—he glanced at his watch—"within the next twenty minutes. I'll be back."

He slammed out and ran down the corridor toward the main dining hall. The passengers still had to be faced—and there was desperately little time to talk to them. No time at all. No time to reason or argue. They had to go at once. He stopped at the next telephone and dialed the number that hooked the phone into the public address system.

"This is the captain speaking. I want every crewman not on duty in the engine room or the control room to report to the main dining hall. *Now*. Within the next sixty seconds." His own voice rasped the words down at him from the speaker above.

Crewmen were already beginning to pile into the dining hall when he reached it, from the entrances on all sides. The tables were slung out of the way, in their between-meals conditions so the floor was clear. One of the passengers was standing on a chair and the others were grouped around him. They looked about in confusion as Don ran up.

"Listen to me," he called out. "I am Lieutenant Chase, the ship's doctor. I am sorry that I cannot explain in detail right now, I will do that later, but it is imperative that you all proceed at *once* to the engine room. . . ."

"We don't want to hear anything from you," the man standing on the chair shouted. "We want the captain and we want an explanation of just what is going on around here."

Don recognized him. Briggs, General Mathew Briggs, re-tired. His close-cropped gray hair gathered itself into spikes, as sharp and hard looking as so much barbed wire. His angry scowl and glowering expression were familiar from the newspapers and news broadcasts. A man who always spoke his opinions, no matter how much they differed from those of the rest of the world, and firmly held opinions they were. Don looked at him coldly and snapped out his words.

"There has been an accident as you know. The captain is dead—as are most of his officers. I am now the acting captain." There were gasps and a sudden stirring among the passengers. "A storm of solar radiation will hit this ship in the next few minutes, and the only safe place will be in the engine room. Everyone will now leave."

There was a movement as the passengers started toward the exits—that stopped as the general called out again.

"Not clear enough and not good enough, Lieutenant. I demand that—"

"You two," Don ordered, jabbing his finger at the nearest crewmen. "Take that man down and haul him to the engine room."

"You cannot do this, hear me—you cannot do this!" the general shouted, backing away, fists raised defensively.

The husky crewmen moved, one to each side—then pounced. The struggle was very brief, and a moment later they half carried the loudly protesting Briggs toward the door.

A thin man, with a large nose and crisp mustache, stepped forward as though to intervene, but stopped when the nearest crewmen started toward him. The rest of the passengers milled about and there was a worried mutter of voices.

"There may be a panic," the purser said in a low voice that only Don could hear.

"I know that, but we have no time for complicated explanations now. We'll have to move them out, quickly and quietly." Don took a thoughtful look around the dining hall. "We have about one crewman here for every ten passengers. I'll go ahead. You get by the door and tell them that the crewmen will show them the way. Break them up into groups like that, ten and one. The crewmen should have a calming influence. There are two elevators to the midpipe, so send alternate groups to the different elevators."

"A very good idea, Captain. . . ." But Don was gone before he could finish.

Don caught up with General Briggs and his attentive guards at the elevator.

"You will regret this," Briggs said with icy fierceness when Don stepped in. He shrugged off the guards' hands as the door slid shut.

"I'm very sorry, General, but I had no other choice. This is an emergency and there was no time to argue. I hope that you will accept my apology. . . ."

"I will *not*. You have started this trouble, mister, and I intend to finish it. There are courts of law."

"That's your choice," Don answered as the elevator stopped and the door opened. Don and the crewmen held to rails on the elevator walls, but Briggs floundered helplessly in midair as his feet rose from the ground.

"Help the general, will you," Don said.

With practiced skill the spacemen grasped the general's arms and kicked off down the midpipe. Don followed, more slowly, and holding onto the rods as he went. He was not as used to free fall as they were. There was no gravity in the ship, but only the sensation of gravity caused by the rotation of the spacer. Here, in the midpipe at the axis of rotation, the centrifugal force was canceled out.

The thick door of the engine room swung open when they

came up to it and the first engineer was waiting, as unsmiling as the general.

"Bringing passengers in here will interrupt our work. It is dangerous," Holtz said.

"I'm sure of that," Don answered, trying to calm him. "But there will be plenty of crewmen to help. Post them at all the controls and danger points. It will be crowded and uncomfortable—but everyone will be alive."

The first passengers began to arrive, some of them tumbling end over end, helpless in free fall. An elderly woman had a distinctly green complexion; she would probably be the first of very many. A crewman rushed a plastic sack to her before there was an accident.

The far wall, at the base of the engines, was filled by the shining control boards, but most of the space in between was free. There was not enough floor space for everyone, so they would have to float in the air. It would be crowded, messy, and uncomfortable. Don got out before there were any more complaints.

When the next load of passengers arrived he rode back up in the empty elevator, sinking back to the floor as he reached the higher decks. He started for the control room at a run. One problem had been licked, the passengers were safe, but the bigger problem remained. Automatically he looked at his watch and felt his skin crawl as he realized that there were only thirteen minutes left until the full force of the storm hit. Thirteen! He ran.

"Just about finished, Captain," Chief Kurikka reported. He was bent over the open control console with a smoking soldering iron. Cables snaked out of it and crossed the floor to vanish through a hole that had been drilled in the metal wall. The chief soldered the last connection and straightened up.

"It should work," he said, and led the way to the washroom. "We've got a couple of hand controllers in there, put them in plastic bags like you said, easiest way to waterproof them. And there's a monitor screen hooked into the stern pickup." They brushed by a man who was smearing a gray paste onto the frame of the open door.

"Silicone putty. The door will be waterproof now when it is closed into the putty seal. The air will exhaust through the vent while the room fills. The spacesuit is there. I'm volunteering to man the station, Captain."

"Very well. We have nine minutes left. Send the other men away as soon as they're finished. Is there any way to tell what the radiation count is while in here?"

Kurikka pointed at the monitor screen—which was one of the TV phones that had been ripped from its mounting and wired to the wall inside another plastic bag.

"The computer is displaying a readout in the bottom of the screen. Those numbers there, below the sun, are the radiation count on the Hoyle scale."

"One point four, not too high yet—no, it just jumped to two point one."

"Fringe of the storm. It's going to be pretty unhealthy in here soon. I think you better get going, sir."

They were alone, the last technician had bolted for the safety of the engine room. Six minutes to go.

"Seal up the suit for me, Chief, then move. That's an order."

"But . . . !" The chief was shocked.

"And no buts either. Your technical knowledge is far

more important to the survival of the ship than my medical
know-how. And as commanding officer I *order* you below."

Kurikka wasted no time in arguing then. He helped Don
into the suit and sealed it. Don grabbed the chief's wrist and
looked at his watch. Two minutes!

He almost shoved the man from the small room, then
pushed on the door while the Chief pulled from the outside,
struggling against the pressure of the putty in the jamb. The
lock finally clicked home and the chief ran. Don was alone.
He turned the faucets full on in the sink and the shower:
someone had plugged all the drains. The water burbled over
the sink edge and splashed to the floor. He turned back to
the monitor screen. The sun had shifted from the cross hairs
on the center and he fired the jet to realign it before he
glanced at the numbers below.

2.8.

The storm was growing in violence.

The sun drifted off center and Don automatically made the
correct adjustments. It looked so small and unimpressive on
the TV screen, a glowing ball more than 100 million miles
away. Yet a storm was raging there now, sending up immense
flares of burning gas heated to over six million degrees centi-
grade. The figure was too big to be grasped. But the reality
could be understood easily enough. First radio waves and
then X rays had been hurled out by the explosions, and had
passed the Earth just eight minutes later. They carried their
warning that the expanding cloud of burning plasma was on
the way. Minutes later the storm of high energy protons
had arrived, the first fringes of the violence to come. Then,
some hours after this, the low energy protons followed, the
very fury of the storm itself. Accelerated particles that could
burn and kill. . . . Don looked away from the imaged sun

and the rising radiation count, to the water that now lapped as high as his ankles.

It wasn't rising fast enough.

And the count was up to 3.2 now. The metal walls of the ship still offered him some protection, but just barely. He wondered if the others were all safe in the engine room. There was a radio switch on the side of his helmet, but when he flicked it he heard only static. Of course, the suit radio would be useless inside this room, where the walls would stop any signal. And, in the last minutes' rush, no one had thought to hook up a telephone circuit. He was alone, cut off.

The water reached his knees—and the numbers on the screen began to blur and climb. . . . 3.9 . . . 4.2 . . . 5.5 . . .

The full force of the storm had hit!

Don dropped the control handles and dived into the water, face down. He had to clutch onto the sink base to hold himself under, as the air in the suit tried to force him to the surface. There was just barely enough water to cover him. It took all the strength of his arms to keep from bobbing up. He fought grimly, knowing that invisible death filled the air above. He *had* to stay down.

The water rose, with painful slowness, and he wondered how far the ship had drifted off course. He would be killing himself if he raised his head to look. He might be killing them all if he didn't. How long had he been under? How long did he dare stay away from the controls? The chief had said that the radiation bulkhead was big enough to protect the engine room if they drifted ten, even fifteen degrees off course. That meant that the sun's image could move almost to the edge of the monitor screen without endangering the people in the ship. But how long would that take? He had no way of knowing, or of measuring elapsed time. What could he do—what *should* he do?

Now the water was high enough so that he could turn over onto his back and half sit up. Through the troubled surface above he could just make out the bulk of the TV repeater in the brightly lit room. He could not see details. It was tantalizingly close now, no more than a foot above his head.

He *had* to look. The others depended on him. *Now!* Yet he would be committing suicide if he put his head above the water.

Perhaps not the entire helmet. He leaned his head back in the helmet, as far as it would go, then slowly raised up. Carefully . . . the surface was right before his face . . . then there was only a thin film of water on the transparent faceplate.

The water ran off from the center, leaving a clear area, and he could see the screen and the dangling control handles.

The sun's image was off-center, almost halfway to the edge of the screen.

The count on the Hoyle scale read 8.7.

The water closed over him as he pushed himself down, deep down. With a maximum possible reading of 10 this solar storm was as strong as any he had ever heard of. The water rose with painful slowness.

When he looked again the count was 9.3 and the sun was at the edge of the screen. He had to move the ship.

The surface of the water wrinkled and he saw that two plastic bags were floating above him. The control handles, of course! Moving carefully he managed to pinch the plastic between his gloved fingers, then dragged the handles down on the end of their lengths of cable. Holding them securely he raised his faceplate up again and found that, if he made no sudden motions, he could work the jet and swing the ship into perfect alignment again.

"We've done it!" he shouted, but his voice only echoed back at him from inside the helmet, reminding him how alone he was. He did not try to speak again.

With the peril over he felt suddenly tired—and he knew this was no time to be tired. As worn out as he was he had to stay awake and alert. He was safe enough in the water, but everyone else depended upon him for their lives. The water level moved upward. It passed the TV screen and rose higher. When it reached the ceiling and began to flow out into the air conditioning vent he turned off all the faucets. The tension was over and now the waiting began. He blinked and wished he could rub his gritty eyes. . . .

An indeterminate time later he realized with sudden shock that he had fallen asleep—and did not know how long he had been asleep. The sun's image was touching the edge of the screen. His hands shook as he brought it safely back to the junction of the cross hairs. The count was holding steady at 8.7. Lower than the maximum, but just as deadly.

How long was the storm going to last? It must have been going on for hours already. For the first time he was concerned about his oxygen supply. The suit was unfamiliar, he had never worn this particular type before, and he had to fumble with the controls on his chest until he hit the right button. The projected dial display appeared to float outside his helmet, in the water.

The oxygen tank was three-quarters empty.

After this he was no longer sleepy. He worked the controls automatically, keeping the ship correctly orientated. It was moving less and less all the time as the different motions were canceled out, one by one.

8.6. The count was dropping, but ever so slowly. His oxygen was being used up even faster. Don breathed as shallowly as he could, and limited his movements. This reduced his oxygen intake. Yet the tank level crept slowly toward the zero mark. He knew that there was still a reserve left after the indicated zero level, but even this would eventually be used up. What should he do then? Choose the manner of his death? From either anoxia or radiation poisoning. The worst part was that there are almost no symptoms of oxygen starvation. The victim just loses consciousness. And dies.

7.6. He would have to estimate the oxygen level remaining, then at the last moment drain the water out of the room enough to open his helmet.

6.3. Soon now. It was past the zero, had been reading zero for a long time. How long? How long was long . . . ?

5.4. Time to drain the water . . . water . . . water . . .

The controls dropped from his hands and he floated limply, oxygen starved, unconscious.

Sliding down the dark tunnel to death.

6

"Is he moving?" the voice asked.

"I think so," another voice answered. "He's coming around."

Don felt he knew who the men were who were speaking, but he could not see them. Realization finally penetrated that they were talking about him. It took a positive effort of will, but he finally opened his eyes. He was on a bed in his own sick bay, and inside an oxygen tent. Bent over the thin plastic was the worried face of First Engineer Holtz, with Rama Kusum next to him.

"Finally got yourself a patient, Rama," Don said, and was shocked at the weakness of his voice. What was he doing here? Sudden memory returned and he tried to sit up.

"What happened? I must have passed out. . . ."

"Take it slowly, sir," Rama said, gently but firmly pressing him back to the pillows. "Everything is in the green. We monitored the radiation count in the engine room, and as soon as it was low enough the chief and I put on the armored suits. We really did soak down the control room getting in to you. By then the count was low enough to take you out of your suit. It was a close one, but as far as I can tell from the diagnostic machine you are fine now."

Don's mind was still unclear, his thoughts muffled.

"What made you come after me?" he asked. "How did you know I was in trouble?"

"The stern pickup was displayed upon the engine room screen. There were some most difficult minutes there, in the beginning, when we thought you had lost control. But you did take care of everything. Then, when the storm was almost over we saw the sun drift right off the screen. That's when we came after you." He smiled. "So you see it has all worked out just fine, everything is all right now. . . ."

As though to mock his words the alarm siren sounded from the PA speaker and the emergency light began to flash brightly.

"FIRE WARNING . . . FIRE WARNING . . ." the recorded voice of the computer said. "THERE IS A FIRE IN COMPART-MENT 64A."

Don tried to get up, then realized how sick he was. He would be a liability in any emergency. He had to delegate authority.

"Holtz—see what you can do about this, then report to me. Rama, take an emergency medical kit and go with him in case anyone has been injured. Could it be equipment failure . . . ?"

At the door, First Engineer Holtz turned and snorted. "None of *my* equipment—64A is a passenger cabin."

Don felt too tired to face any more crises, but he knew he had to. Sitting up was an effort, but he finally did it. He switched off the oxygen, then had to wait a moment to regain some bit of strength. Fire. Just as if the ship's oxygen supply wasn't bad enough already. And their orbit, he had to think about that now. Everyone had forgotten about it during the solar storm. If they didn't find a way of correcting course soon it would be too late—and they would go right on past Mars and into the eternity of interstellar space. The phone rang. He reached out and painfully picked it up.

"Captain here," he said automatically, no longer self-conscious about using the title. Chief Kurikka looked out of the tiny screen.

"Captain, is First Engineer Holtz there? There has been a report of a fire. . . ."

"I know. He's taking care of it. Where are you now?"

"In the control room, sir, taking temporary command. The thing is that we are getting more reports on smoke throughout A deck. We can't tell yet if there are other fires, or if the smoke from 64A is being spread by the ventilation system. Request permission to seal and cut off air circulation in A deck and clear the deck."

"Permission granted. Contact me here as soon as you hear anything else."

Don hung up the phone and rose, slowly, to his feet. Ignoring the swimming sensation this caused, he walked to the door and leaned on the handle for a moment before opening it. He was in the isolation room that opened directly into his office. The drug cabinet was on the far wall. By the time he reached it he was walking a little better. He put his thumb on the identification plate and the lock clicked open: it would open only to the pattern of his thumbprint. There were potent drugs here that would mask his fatigue and supply the energy to carry on. He did not like to use them—and he would pay for it later with an even greater fatigue reaction—but at this moment he had no choice. The glass vial slipped into the barrel of the spray hypodermic, and he gave himself the injection. The phone rang while he was closing the drug cabinet.

It was Kurikka again and this time, if possible, his glum expression was deeper than ever.

"Air circulation stopped and deck sealed. All passengers evacuated. I've sent some men to help. But—can you get over there, sir? They need a doctor."

"What for?"

"Sounds like smoke poisoning."

"I'm on my way."

The drug was taking effect: Don felt lightheaded, but strong enough to walk around now. There was oxygen in the emergency medical kit that Rama had taken, but they might need more. He unclipped a tank and mask from the wall and hurried out.

There were airtight doors sealing off A deck, but they were unlocked, and opened when he came close. Inside there was a haze in the air and a nose-smarting reek of smoke. A man was lying on the deck before compartment 64A and Rama was bent over him, holding an oxygen mask to his face. Rama was coughing heavily, and his face and hands were smeared with soot. When he came closer Don saw that the prone man was the first engineer.

"Had to . . . break the door down. . . ." Rama wheezed, between racking coughs. "Filled with smoke . . . thought someone might be in there. . . ."

"Don't talk any more," Don ordered. "Use this oxygen on yourself. I'll take over here."

Don was afraid. He snapped the strap of the oxygen mask into place, then used his thumb to pull back the lid of one of Holtz's closed eyes. Bad. He took the man's pulse with one hand while he rummaged in the emergency medical kit with the other. He found the Syrette he wanted, pressed it to the side of the engineer's neck, and triggered the injection. Rama was watching, and he took the oxygen mask from his face long enough to speak.

"That was a shot of Alkavervir," he said. "A cardiovascular stimulant. That means he has—"

"Heart trouble. Right. Not many people knew about it. That's why he is retiring after this trip."

"How is he?"

"Not good. This is the worst kind of thing that could have happened to him. Was there anyone in the compartment?"

"No. No one that we could see. Then the smoke got to us."

A crewman came out of the compartment door with a heavy-duty fire extinguisher, the nozzle still slowly burbling foam.

"In the green, sir. The fire's out."

Don stood and looked in at the ruins of the cabin. The walls were scorched and streaked with smoke, and foam was everywhere. Two sodden heaps of charred debris were on the floor.

"How could it possibly burn?" Don asked. "I thought these ships were virtually fireproof."

"They are. But the luggage wasn't. Two suitcases, clothes and contents burned up."

"Do you have any idea how it started?"

The crewman hesitated, then held out his hand. "I don't want to make any charges, Captain, but I found this on the table."

In his hand was a sodden package of cigarettes. Don looked at them in silence for a moment, his jaw tightening.

"Take them to Chief Kurikka and give him a complete

report about what happened here," Don said. "But call him in control first and have him get two men here with a stretcher at once."

"Doctor," Rama called out. "Come quickly. I think his pulse is getting irregular."

Don took one look and shouted to the crewman. "Hold that call. Help us. We have to get this man to the sick bay at once."

First Engineer Carl Holtz was no longer a young man, and his heart trouble had been coming on for years. He responded well to the medication and treatment, but the sick bay, though well equipped, lacked some things that were commonplace in a planet-based hospital. There was no heart-lung machine for one thing. And of course no surgical team to stand by in case a transplant might be called for. But Don did his best with what he had. Rama Kusum, despite his protests, was put to bed himself because of the smoke poisoning. Four beds of the small ward were now occupied.

Two hours later Don called the control room for a report: he was a doctor, but was commanding officer of the spaceship as well.

"All localized," Kurikka reported. "No other fires, no other smoke damage outside of that compartment."

"What about our oxygen?"

"Down some, but nothing major. At the moment. I poked through the mess and found that there was a burned cigarette in it. Looks like it fell out of the ashtray and set the luggage on fire."

Don thought a moment. "Is there a brig on this ship?" he asked.

Kurikka's eyes opened wider at the question, but his answer was crisply exact.

"In a manner of speaking, Captain. Compartment 84B can be locked from the outside and not opened from the inside. It's been used as a brig before."

"Fine. I want you to find the occupant of that burned compartment and lock him or her up. These people must be made to understand how serious our situation is. If whoever it was had not disobeyed the order about smoking this would never have happened."

"Well, sir, if you knew who the occupant was—"

"I couldn't care less! That was an order, Chief."

"Immediate action will be taken, sir. Could I ask—how is Commander Holtz? I heard he breathed a lot of that smoke."

Don looked at the figure on the bed across the room.

"First Engineer Holtz is dead," he said. "Keep that information to yourself for the moment. I don't wish it to be common knowledge yet that we have lost our only remaining engineering officer."

7

The effects of the stimulants were wearing off and Don was exhausted and grim. He certainly had reason to be. He looked around the wardroom, at the faces of the worried men, and if he hadn't been so depressed he might have laughed. The officers of the interplanetary spacer *Johannes Kepler* left a certain amount to be desired.

A captain who was a doctor—and who had never set foot inside a spaceship until a few weeks ago.

A second officer who was only a chief petty officer. Yet probably the most valuable man aboard at this moment.

A technical adviser who was a civilian and a mathematician of some genius, but who was so unworldly he made mistakes in addition.

A frightened atomic engineering mate, second class, who was now in charge of the engines of a two billion dollar spacecraft.

Don poured another cup of coffee and tried not to sigh. He looked at the engineering mate and forced himself to smile.

"Congratulations, Tyblewski, you're the acting first engineer of the Big Joe."

Tyblewski was a small blond man, unmemorable in any way—other than by his large ears, which protruded like jug handles from the sides of his head. He was chewing his lower lip nervously.

"I don't know, sir," he said. "I'm just an atomic rating. I can follow orders, but—"

"Then you'll follow this order," Don broke in. "The chief tells me that you know your work and that you are the only one aboard this ship that is in any way qualified to look after the engines. You *will* do that job."

Tyblewski opened his mouth, as if to speak, then shut it again. He nodded his head in mute agreement. Don hated to play the role of the bully, but he had no choice. The ship— and the passengers—must come first.

"All right, gentlemen," Don said, looking around the circle, "I am going to outline our position as it stands now. The solar storm has passed and we can forget about it. The oxygen situation is not dangerous—*at the moment*. That means that we lost a lot of the phytoplankton when we lost the water, so the oxygen concentration is falling slowly inside the ship. It is not at a dangerous level yet, so we can put that difficulty aside for the moment. The most pressing problem is our course. A major correction is long overdue. If we stay on this course we shall miss Mars by a good million miles and keep on going. Dr. Ugalde, could we have your report."

The dark-haired mathematician was sunk in gloom; his forehead was wrinkled and incised lines pulled at the corners of his mouth. He raised his hands, palms upward, in a gesture of despair.

"What can I say? Would lying help? I have done my best—and I am afraid that it is wanting, not good enough. In theory I can navigate this great ship. The mathematics are simple. But in practice it is beyond me. I am studying the navigator's books, but it will take a long time. I must learn the correct programming for the computer, another major problem. . . ." He shrugged his shoulders again. Don exercised more control over his voice than he really felt.

"Could you tell me, Doctor, just how long it will take to gain the knowledge."

"Weeks! Months! I cannot say. I beg your forgiveness. I will keep studying."

Not good enough, Don thought to himself. We don't have the time.

"Then we had better think about the radio," he said aloud. "Sparks has raided the spare parts stores, and he and Electrician's Mate Gold are jury-rigging a transmitter. The receiver he put together is working better now, but there is still enough sunspot activity to lower the quality of the reception. This will make things even worse for the transmitter because we do not have the power to punch through the interference. However, it is about all we can do. Do any of you have anything to bring up here?"

"Two things, sir."

"What are they, Kurikka?"

"The matter of the captain's . . . of Captain Kardyd's funeral. There hasn't been time to think about it up until now."

"If you will make the arrangements we'll do that as soon as possible."

"Everything's done. Just waiting for the word from you."

"Right after this meeting, then. What was the second matter?"

"The prisoner in the brig, he's protesting. He wants to talk to you."

"Our arsonist! I'll admit I had forgotten all about him. I never even asked you his name."

"It's . . . General Mathew Briggs, sir."

"I might have known. It makes no difference in any case. He's there and he's going to stay there. I'll talk to him when I get a chance."

There were no other questions and Don closed the meeting. The burial of Captain Kardyd was to take place in one hour's time. The announcement was made throughout the ship. Don rested on his bunk until fifteen minutes before the ceremony. He tried to sleep, but could not. The urgency of their situation kept his thoughts twisting and stirring. He wished, not for the first time, that someone else had this job that he had so reluctantly accepted. He was doing his best, but the situation kept deteriorating. Perhaps it was time to admit that the ship had really been destroyed by that meteorite, that all the patchwork and effort were doomed from the very beginning. They were all dead . . . why didn't they admit it. . . .

The shrill buzz of the alarm jerked him awake. He had drifted into a half sleep where all his worst fears had become real. Were they real? He shook himself, trying to rid himself of the feeling of black depression, but it would not go.

A shower helped, first steaming hot, then cold. The water was replaced by a comforting flow of warmed air. When he was dry, he put on his dress uniform and went to the service airlock on A deck. The others were assembled and awaiting him. He returned Kurikka's salute.

"All present, sir," he reported. "The burial party is standing by, and the ship's company is fallen in. All watch-keeping stations are manned." He produced a black-bound

book with a cloth marker in it, and continued in a low voice
that only Don could hear.

"I'll handle the ceremony, it's not very long. When I call
the company to attention, hats off, you read the part here
in the ship's regulations where I have the slip."

"Carry on, Chief."

It was a simple, but moving, ceremony that undoubtedly
had roots in the ancient ritual of burial at sea. The spaceship's
company, almost forty of them, every man in the ship outside
of the minimum number of men on duty, stood at attention
while the flag-draped body of the captain was carried forward
to the measured beat of a drum. Only a handful of passengers
had elected to watch: they had been near enough to death
recently and perhaps did not wish to be reminded of it.
Six men carried the body, and placed it down gently next
to the round spacelock that was set into the deck.

"Hats off," the chief petty officer ordered. There was a
rustle as the men took off their headgear. Don put his hat
under his arm and stepped forward with the open book in
his hand.

"We entrust unto the deeps of space this man, Captain
Kardyd, commanding officer of the *Johannes Kepler,* who was
a sailor of these trackless seas. . . ."

The ritual was not long, just a page of words in a book,
yet as Don read it he knew that it was more than that.
Kardyd had commanded one of the greatest vessels of all
time, sailing a course that was measured in millions, not
hundreds, of miles. He had been struck down by chance,
but his ship and his crew lived on. They would do their
jobs, to the very end if necessary, just as the captain had
done. And he, Donald Chase, M.D., of the United States of
America, Earth, had become a part of this. He had gone to

space not completely knowing the responsibilities he had taken on, nor the comradeship he would be joining. He did now. He finished reading and looked up at the men—who looked back at him as one of them. It was a moment that Don knew he would never be able to forget.

"Hats on, burial party forward."

There was the whir of motors, the hiss of oiled metal on metal, and the inner lock of the spacelock rose up. The bearers stepped forward, climbing down the ladders with their burden, to place it on the outer door below, which formed the floor of the cylindrical compartment. When they emerged they carried, carefully folded, the blue and white Earth flag. The inner door closed and the pumps throbbed as they exhausted the air.

"Would you actuate the outer lock, Captain," Kurikka said, and stepped away from the controls.

Don stood beside him and waited until the ready light flashed on. Then he touched the button that, soundlessly in the vacuum, opened the outer lock. The centrifugal force of the ship's rotation would carry the body out and away from the ship on a constantly diverging course.

"Dismiss."

Don turned away, exhausted, and started for his quarters. He had not gone a dozen steps before he heard footsteps running after him.

"Captain, sir, could I see you?"

It was Sparks. There was grease on his hands and face and sooty hollows of fatigue under his eyes. He had not slept in a very long time. He remembered Don's orders not to discuss ship's affairs before the passengers, and followed him in silence to the control room.

"We've fixed up a transmitter," he said as soon as the door was closed.

"Wonderful! Now let's see if we can raise Mars Central."

The receiver was muttering in the background, turned low since Mars Central was broadcasting a taped recording on their ship's frequency. It repeated, over and over, that scheduled contacts had not been received, and would the *Kepler* report at once. Sparks turned up the receiver volume so they would hear at once if their message was received, and the recorded transmission interrupted.

"Doesn't look like much," Electrician's Mate Gold admitted, "but it works fine."

"Just not very powerful," Sparks admitted, looking at the collection of parts spread on the table before them. There was a replacement unit from the radar, the amplifier stage from the wardroom hi-fi tape deck, and even some components from the electronic ovens. Wires and wave ducts crawled through the breadboard jumble and a heavy cable snaked out to the power supply.

"Are you sure it's putting out a signal?" Don asked.

"Absolutely," Sparks said, and made a careful adjustment on the variable condensers. "I've set it onto our reception frequency. The broadcast signal will be picked up on our receiving aerial. I've got the gain turned way down."

He flicked on the microphone and whispered into it. His words boomed out of the receiver, drowning out the message from Mars.

"Sounds pretty strong to me," Don said.

"Yeah." Gold was very gloomy. "But we just broadcast from the antenna to the aerial, maybe 100 feet. We got how many million miles to Mars?"

"But they have some great receivers there," Sparks said

defensively. "They got a parabolic dish antenna that can pick up a signal—"

"That's enough," Don said. "Let's see if we can get through."

Word must have gone out, because Kurikka came in with Dr. Ugalde, and Purser Jonquet hurried up soon after them. Sparks made painfully exact adjustments on the frequency, testing the signal over and over before he was satisfied. He turned the power full on, then pulled the microphone to him. He coughed self-consciously once, then flipped on the transmission switch.

"*Johannes Kepler* calling Mars Central . . . come in, Mars Central . . . how do you read me? Come in . . ."

He repeated the call, over and over, in patient clear tones. The receiver with its taped message droned accompaniment to his words. Then he flicked off the power and leaned back. There was no change in the message they were receiving.

"It's not getting through?" Don asked.

"Too early to tell yet, sir. At these distances it takes a couple of minutes for our signal to get there, and the same amount of time for theirs to get back." He turned on the set and began calling again.

The taped message did not change, while the big red second hand of the clock on the bulkhead continued its slow sweeps.

Minutes passed. No one wanted to ask the question and the silence was worse than words. It was Sparks who finally broke the spell. He dropped the mike and flipped off the power supply. When he turned they saw that his face was beaded with sweat.

"I'm sorry, Captain, but it's no go. Our signal is getting out—but it just isn't strong enough. There is still plenty of background noise from the storm, and we're not punching through it. . . ."

He stopped as the tape recorded message cut off, and there was a moment of hushed silence before a new voice came on.

"*Johannes Kepler*—are you broadcasting? We have been picking up traces of a signal on your frequency, but cannot read your signal. Are you broadcasting? Repeat—can you hear me? This is Mars Central calling the *Johannes Kepler*. We have a very weak signal on your frequency but cannot read it. . . ."

"It's the storm," Sparks explained, "that and the low power. . . ."

"You did your best, Sparks," Don told him. "No one is blaming you."

There was no one who could be blamed.

But that did not help.

If they could not contact Mars they were as good as dead at this moment.

8

The others had turned away, but Don was looking at the crude transmitter, glaring at it, as though he could force it to work just by strength of will alone. There had to be a way—and this radio was the only hope they had left.

"Isn't there any way you can increase the power?" he asked.

Sparks shook his head. "I've already got all the circuits on a forty percent overload. They can take that for a while without burning out. You saw, I kept cutting the current every few minutes. Any more and they would pop as soon as I turned on the juice."

"Are there any other ways you can beef up the circuits?"

"Negative on that, I'm afraid. Wiring up this thing was the easiest job. Me and Gold spent most of the time seeing what was the best circuit we could get out of the junk we could find. But the signal will improve as we get closer to Mars. They'll hear us eventually."

"Eventually is a word that is not too good," Ugalde said. He came up next to the radio and stood, rocking on his toes with his hands behind his back, as though he were addressing a class. "Now while I admit with great chagrin that being a navigator is impossible for me at this moment, I am still yet able to calculate an orbit. Roughly mind you, but I have worked it out as best I can from the figures of the last calculations made by the deceased navigator. Our course error grows greater with every passing moment, and the greater the error the harder it is to correct. If I may give an analogy. Imagine, if you will, a very long, wide slope, down which a ball is rolling. If the ball rolls straight down it will strike a stick standing at the foot of the slope. Now, if the ball is deflected by a slight push, it will roll at a slightly diverging angle from the true course. But a slight push will set it straight so it hits the stick after all. A slight push *soon* after the deflection. If the correction is not made at once, after a period of time the ball will be rolling many feet away from the proper course, and a really hard blow will be needed to correct it. The longer the wait, the more force that is needed. Of course you realize the ball is our ship, Mars the hypothetical stick. We have delayed a long time already. If we wait too much longer we may not be able to make the corrections that will bring us back to the proper way. Contact must be established with Mars—and at once."

Nothing could be said after this, and the air of gloom in the control room was thick enough to be cut with a knife. Sparks looked around, from face to face, pulling back against the table.

"Don't look at me!" he called out loudly, defensively. "I've done all I could with the parts we had. I built a radio and it works, you heard that. It's putting out all it can. There's nothing more I can do. It's a working radio, don't forget that, with a modulated signal, not a radar or a signal generator where you just blast out. This is all we've got—"

Don took him by the shoulder, harder than he intended, his fingers digging deep. "What was that you said about radar?" He let go quickly when he saw the man's shocked expression.

"It's nothing, sir. Nothing to do with us. If you just squirt out a signal you can get maybe twice the power we have going out now. But we have to modulate the signal to carry information. Otherwise Mars Central will be getting nothing but a blast of static from our direction. They'll know that we're still here—but that's about all they will know."

"No!" Don said. "There's more." He paced back and forth, driving his fist into the palm of his hand. "Something can be done. I know, I read about it once, a book or something like that, about the early days of radio. Something about code. . . ."

"Sure," Sparks answered. "Code. They used to use it maybe a couple of hundred years ago. We had it in history at radio school. Before they could modulate a signal to carry a message they used to just blast it out, then interrupt it in short or long bits in a regular kind of code. I guess they had a special signal for every letter. Then at the other end they would put it back into letters again. But we can't do that—"

"Why not?"

Sparks started to smile, then changed his mind when he saw the expression on Don's face. "Well, you see . . . no one knows the code any more. So even if we knew it and could send it, no one could read it. It would be a great idea if we could do it, but—"

"No buts. We'll do it. Could you transmit the long and short signals if I gave you a message?"

"Well, I guess so. I could rig a make-or-break switch and

keep opening and closing it. Or we could record it on tape, that might be easier, and have the taped signal actuate a relay. I guess, mechanically, it could be done."

"Then do it. I'll bring you back the message as soon as I can. Get your equipment rigged. Kurikka, come with me."

The chief didn't speak until they were out in the corridor; then he let out the breath he had been holding.

"Would you mind, sir, telling me just what you have in mind." He looked baffled and Don almost laughed.

"It's easy. We're going to the library. The information will be there. If not in the shelved books it will be in the library's memory."

It really was easy after that. None of the books, they were mostly fiction for the passengers' entertainment, looked promising, so Don punched for the encyclopedia index. CA-CU had an entry marked *codes* and he tried three or four sub-entries before he found an article on the International Code. It contained a copy of the code itself.

"There it is," Don said, pointing at the columns of letters and dots and dashes. He pressed the *print* button. "Now let's see if we can transcribe a message in this stuff."

Back in the control room, it was the mathematician, Dr. Ugalde, who suggested the solution.

"The computer, we must give it instructions. This is the kind of operation the stupid machine is built for. If you will permit I will program the computer to transform a typed message into this code and it will then record the code on tape for the transmitter. The message will be transmitted and, I am sure, it will be quickly comprehended that it is a code. I suggest that, before the message, we transmit the numbers from one to ten, counting in dots to make the series, that is. This will indicate that there is intelligent content

in the broadcast, not just a random collection of pulses.
With that clue it will not take them long to figure out
what is happening."

"That sounds fine to me," Don said. "After the numbers
send a simple message, just ask them if they can understand
the code so that we can send more detailed messages.
Tell them we can hear their voice transmissions, but will
have to answer in code." He turned to the others. "Get this
gear rigged as quickly as possible. I'm going to the sick bay
to look after my patients. Call me as soon as you are ready
to broadcast."

It required his best bedside manner to give optimistic
answers to the questions. Yes, the storm had passed and
there would be no more coming. And, no, there was no
truth in the rumor that they were running out of air. The
air smelled just fine, didn't it? He changed the dressings on
the wounds, released the frostbite case, and told him to return
once a day, then retreated to his quarters as quickly as
possible. The phone rang as he entered and he once more
had to assume the role of captain. The message was ready
to be sent.

"Works in the green on the test," Sparks said, throwing
a switch when Don came in. A slow series of dits and dahs
sounded from the speaker. "We've got the tape working
through this switching circuit. I'm getting an antenna output
almost double what we had before."

"Send it," Don said, and dropped into the captain's chair
before the control panels. Jonquet brought in coffee and
passed the cups around.

Sparks reran the tape and made the necessary adjustments.
The reel spun and the message crackled out into space. The
receiver still repeated the recorded message they had been

getting for days now. Twice Sparks reran the tape and repeated the transmission, before finally switching off the apparatus.

"Just a matter of waiting now," he said.

Dr. Ugalde scribbled some quick calculations on a piece of
paper. "It is my estimate," he said, "considering our probable
position in relation to Mars, that we could hear a return
message in less than thirty seconds from now."

They all looked at the clock, at the sweeping hand. It
seemed to crawl, slower and slower, finally reaching thirty
seconds and passing it. Going on for a minute more. A minute
and a half. Ugalde crumpled his piece of paper.

"Perhaps my mathematics are wrong, an error. . . ."

He broke off as the droning voice from the receiver suddenly ended. They all turned, automatically, looking at the
now silent speaker. There were seconds of silence before a
new voice cut in.

"Hello, *Johannes Kepler* . . . can you hear me? We are
receiving a transmission on your frequency of a series of
pulses. Are you transmitting this? If you are, send five pulses.
Repeat them because reception varies at this end. . . ."

"Do it!" Don ordered.

Sparks had rigged a manual push-button switch into the
circuit. He used it now, sending out the dots, over and over,
five, five, five, five. . . .

Then they waited, once again, the long minutes while
their message, traveling 186,000 miles a second, at the speed
of light, reached out to Mars and was received. Until the
answer was broadcast.

"We have received your message, *Johannes Kepler*," the
voice said, and an impromptu cheer shook the room. ". . .
means you have had difficulty with your radio. Someone here

has just reported that your message is in code and the library is being consulted for a copy. If you believe we have a copy here and will be able to translate your message, please send all details. Repeat your message at least five times, I repeat, send your message at least five times since we are having reception difficulties at this end. We are standing by to receive now, good luck."

It took time, a lot of time, because the communication was so complex. Don typed a message into the computer, explaining what had happened, and this was recorded on tape as a series of dots and dashes. Another tape was prepared of up-to-date stellar observations which were recorded along with the earlier data. The computer on Mars would process these and determine the course corrections that would be needed. Time passed, and with each second they moved further from their proper course.

They waited again and, instead of the course corrections, they received a request for the amount of reaction mass that remained in their tanks. This was sent back as quickly as possible and there were minutes of silence as they waited for the answer, for the corrections that would get them back into the proper orbit for Mars. The message finally came.

"Hello, Big Joe," the voice rasped and, although the man speaking tried to sound happy, there was an undertone of worry in his voice. "We are not saying that this is the final answer, the figures are being rerun, and something will be done. But the truth is . . . well . . . you have been in an incorrect orbit for too long a time. It appears that, with the reaction mass you have remaining . . . there is not enough to make a course correction for Mars. Your ship is on an unchangeable orbit into outer space."

9

In the silence that followed this shocking announcement, the rapping on the control room door sounded unnaturally loud. An air tenders mate came in and saluted, throwing a quick glance around at the silent men. He handed a slip of paper to Don.

"I thought I had better bring these readings directly to you, sir. I just ran the test a few minutes ago."

Don stirred himself, it took an effort to think of other problems after what they had just heard. He took the slip and looked, uncomprehending, at the piece of paper.

"I'm sorry, could you tell me what these figures mean?"

The air tender pointed to the row of numbers on the right, and to the last one, which was circled in red.

"These are the percentages of oxygen concentration in the air. You'll notice they have been going down steadily. These are the figures taken every five hours, since the accident. The change has been slow, but there is now an abrupt drop, here in the last number. I think the radiation from the solar storm knocked out a lot of phytoplankton. That, in addition to what we lost with the water, is putting us below equivalency."

"What does that mean?"

"Well, simply, sir, the people in the ship are turning oxygen into carbon dioxide faster than the plants can replace the oxygen. We're running out of breathable air."

Don shook himself. There were too many problems at once.

"How long before it reaches the danger level?" he asked.

"Days at least, I'm not sure. But something should be done now. . . ."

"Not at the present moment. I'll be down to air control as soon as I can. Who is in charge?"

The crewman, he could not have been over twenty years old, looked uncomfortable. "Well, Lieutenant Hong is dead, so I guess that leaves me."

"What's your name?"

"Hansen, Air Tenders Mate Third Class Hansen."

"All right, Hansen, you are now acting air control officer. Do your work well because we all depend upon you."

"Yes, sir," Hansen said, squaring his back and saluting.

He'll do the job, Don thought, watching the man leave. Then memory of the message from Mars returned, and with it a feeling of sick depression. He turned to Kurikka.

"What is this reaction mass that Mars Central is so worried about?" he asked. "I hate to act stupid, but medical studies leave little time for reading about anything else. I thought this ship was powered by atomic engines?"

"It is, sir, but we still need reaction mass. A rocket moves not by pushing against anything, but by throwing something away. Whatever is thrown away is called reaction mass. In chemical rockets it is burning gas. The gas goes in one direction, the rocket goes in the other. The more you throw away, the more reaction you get and the faster you go. You also get more reaction by throwing something away *faster*. That is what we do. Our reaction mass is made up of finely divided particles of silicon. It's made from steel plant slag, vaporized in a vacuum, so the particles are microscopic. These particles are accelerated by the engines to an incredible speed. That's what gives us our push."

Don nodded. "Seems simple enough—at least in theory. So, although we have unlimited power from the atomic engines, we don't have enough reaction mass for the course change required?"

"Right, sir. Normally we carry more than enough mass for our needs, because the course corrections are made as early as possible. The more the ship gets away from the right orbit, the more mass that is needed to get us back. We've waited a little too long this time."

Don refused to give in to the feeling of gloom that swept the control room.

"Can't we use something else for reaction mass?" he asked.

Kurikka shook his head. "I'm afraid not. Nothing is small enough to get through the injectors. And the engines are designed to run with this kind of reaction mass only." He turned away and, for the very first time, Don saw that the rock-like chief petty officer was feeling defeat. "I'm afraid there is nothing that we can do."

"We *can't* give up!" Don insisted. "If we can't change the orbit to the correct one, we can certainly alter it as much as possible, get it closer to the correct one."

"Maybe we can, Captain, but it won't help. With all our mass used to change course we won't have enough for deceleration."

"Well at least we'll be closer to Mars. There must be other ships there that can match orbits with us and take everyone off. Let's ask Mars Central about it."

The answer was infuriatingly slow in coming, and not very hopeful.

"We are running all the possibilities through the computer here, but there is nothing positive yet. There are no deep-spacers here who can aid you, and the surface to satellite ferries don't have the range to reach you, even with your correct orbit. Don't give up hope, we are still working on the problem."

"Great lot of good that does us," Sparks muttered. "You're not in our shoes."

"I am afraid I must disagree with Chief Kurikka and say that his last statement is wrong," Ugalde said. He had been standing in a daze of concentration for a long time, and did not realize that the chief's "last" statement had been spoken almost fifteen minutes earlier. "There is something we can do. I have examined the situation from all sides and, if you will permit me to point out, you are looking at only part of the problem. This is because you have stated the question wrong." He began to pace back and forth.

"The problem is to alter our orbit to the correct one, not to find more mass. Stated this way the problem becomes clear and the answer is obvious."

"Not to me," Kurikka said, speaking for all of them.

Ugalde smiled. "If we cannot get more reaction mass, then we must get less mass for our present quantity of reaction mass to work against."

Don smiled back. "Of course! That's it! We will just have to lighten ship."

"It is important that everything that is jettisoned be

weighed first," Ugalde warned. "This will be needed in the computations. And the faster it is done the better our chances will be!"

"We start right now," Don said, pulling over a note pad and electric stylo. "I want to list everything that is not essential to the operation of the ship and the lives of everyone aboard. Suggestions?"

"The passengers' luggage of course," Ugalde said. "They should keep what they are wearing and the rest will be discarded."

The purser moaned. "I can see the lawsuits already."

"I'm sure that the company is insured," Don said, making a note. "Their luggage or their lives—that is really not much of a choice. They can keep their valuables and personal items, but anything that can be replaced has to go. You better have them all assembled in the main dining hall in fifteen minutes. I'll come up and tell them myself."

Jonquet nodded and left. Don turned to the others.

"The dining tables, chairs, dishes, most of the kitchen equipment," Kurikka said, counting off the items on his fingers. "All the frozen meat and refrigerated food. We can live off the dehydrated emergency rations which use recycled water."

"Good thinking. Who's next?"

Once they began to concentrate on it, it was amazing the number of items that they found. Carpets and decorations and banisters on the stairs, furniture, fittings, and spare parts. The list grew and Don checked off the items. There was one obvious—and heavy—item missing. "The cargo," he said, "what about that?"

Kurikka shook his head. "I only wish we could. There is heavy machinery, bales of clothing, a lot of items that ·

we could do without. But all the cargo is container loaded for the most part, and sealed into place against the G stresses. The shuttle rockets have the special extensible power sockets to reach down past the containers to free them, but we don't have the equipment. I suppose we could jury-rig something to get the containers out, but it would take a couple of days at least."

"Which is far too long for us. The cargo stays—but everything else that can go, *goes!*"

As the crew got the jettisoning underway, Don went, reluctantly, to the main dining hall. He had some idea of the reception facing him there, and he was not far wrong. The passengers, all 112 of them, were waiting for him, and were in an ugly mood. He had to shout to be heard because of the noise made by the crewmen who were already tearing out the tables. He explained about the difficulties they were experiencing, the fact that they were far off course because of the accident, and the need to lighten ship. A concerted growl of anger went up when he told them that their luggage was being thrown from the ship as well.

"You have no right and you cannot force me to!" an elderly matron called out and there were shouts of agreement from all sides. Don waited until they were silent before he spoke again.

"I am sorry if I appear to be highhanded. But I assure you that there is no other way out of this mess. This is not my decision. You know that I am a doctor, and the acting captain of this ship only because all of the other officers are dead. But we have been in contact with Mars Central and it is *their* decision that we must lighten this ship or we will never be able to turn it." There were more complaints, but Don shouted them down.

"I am captain and this is an order. You will keep only the items I have mentioned, and you *will* bring your luggage here within a half an hour. Your lives depend upon it."

They left, reluctantly, grumbling complaints to one another. Don smiled wryly to himself, thinking that he would never win any popularity polls with these people. But he had to save their lives—whether they liked it or not. One man stayed behind and approached Don. He looked familiar, a lean, tanned man with a crisp mustache. He introduced himself.

"My name is Doyle, Captain, I am General Briggs' secretary."

"Yes. What can I do for you?"

Doyle ignored the sharp edge to Don's voice, and smiled. "Not so much for me, Captain, but for General Briggs. He would like to talk to you. Is that such an unreasonable request?"

Don hesitated. He remembered that he had promised to talk to Briggs. He might as well get it over with, and this would be as good a time as any, while the excess weight was being jettisoned.

"All right, I'll come with you now."

"Thank you, sir, I know that the general will appreciate this."

They stopped by the control room for the key to the compartment, then went to the temporary brig. The general stood up from the bunk when they entered.

"Very good of you to come, Captain," he said.

"You wanted to talk with me, General?"

"Yes, if I could have a minute of your time. But what I really wanted to do was apologize for the incident in my cabin. I, of course, turned in all my cigarettes, I can take orders as well as give them, you know. However I forgot one pack which, completely without thinking, I started to smoke. That is the cause of the accident. I am very sorry that it happened."

"So are we, General."

"I am sure of that. Now, if I may, I would like to ask you how long you plan to keep me in this compartment? I am not protesting my sentence, your actions were completely justified, but I do feel that the term of the punishment should be spelled out."

Don thought quickly. He needed the passengers' cooperation, and having the general on his side would surely help. The man's earlier anger was gone and he seemed genuinely repentant. There was no point at all in keeping him locked up any longer.

"You're free to go now, General. This was never a matter of punishment, just a temporary measure until we uncovered the reason for the fire."

"Very kind of you."

The last words were cold and formal, with none of the warmth the general had shown while explaining a moment earlier. He and Doyle turned and left at once. Don looked after them, some memory gnawing at him. What was it the crewman had said? Wasn't it something about there being more cigarettes in the burned luggage? Well, even if the general had lied to get out of confinement, it was not important. The incident was closed and he had the ship to think about.

As he descended the stairway to A deck he saw an incredible sight. Since the floor of this deck was the outer skin of the ship, tempered glass viewing ports were set into the floor. They were two yards in diameter and framed circles of blackest space, punctured by the bright, unflickering light of the myriad stars. The stars appeared to move by steadily, as the ship rotated to provide weight for the passengers. Except at the times of arrival and departure the stars were the only thing that could be seen.

Not any more. The brilliant light of the distant sun, unshielded by any atmosphere, glinted from the many objects that streamed through space around the ship. Tables, suitcases, chairs, hams, shoes, rugs, rails, cans, crockery, the list was endless. They moved slowly away, appearing to shrink and vanish, and new objects took their place. The jettisoning had begun.

The scene around the airlock was that of orderly confusion. A counterbalance scale had been rigged next to the open door of the lock. As the miscellany of things to be discarded arrived they were weighed, and the weight recorded, then were unceremoniously dumped into the open mouth of the lock. When the level reached up to the opening, the door was closed and the air pumped out. Then the outer door opened and centrifugal force hurled everything out to join the stream of debris moving slowly away. When the airlock was closed the entire routine was repeated. Chief Kurikka was supervising the operation, and he came to report as soon as he saw Don.

"Going well so far, Captain. We have had some trouble with the passengers, but that is going smoothly now too."

"What kind of trouble?"

The chief looked around, then lowered his voice.

"I'm a realistic man, sir, and when my life depends upon it I am not one to think much about applying the honor system. I've had the purser and some of the men going through their cabins after the passengers have dumped their luggage. We've found a lot of 'essential' items that weren't that essential. They've been dumped too."

"You're a hard man, Chief, and there will be lawsuits to prove it. But I'll back you all the way."

"Yes, sir. We're just about through here and the weight we discarded is being totaled for Mars Central."

"Finish as quickly as possible. You know why."

Kurikka nodded silently and went back to his work. Don turned away—and stumbled. He had to grab the wall for support. He was tired beyond belief, but he could not stop until the course corrections had been made. Walking, slowly and carefully, he went along the passageway to the control room where he fell into the captain's chair.

"Firing information is in, sir," a voice said—and Don jerked his head up. He had dozed off without even knowing it. He blinked at the sheet of paper that Sparks held out to him.

"What do they say?"

"Ten minutes to blast. The chief and Dr. Ugalde are setting up the sequence. Mars Central says that they are 'optimistic' about the course change now."

"They better be right as well as optimistic," Don grumbled. "Thanks, Sparks, you—the entire crew—have done a great job on this."

"Hope it works, sir," he said, putting down the paper and turning away.

The machines took over. The computer on Mars had worked out the firing instructions for the course change, and the figures were fed into the ship's computer. Once it knew the correct attitude desired, the computer fired the positioning jet and tilted the great ship in space. Don looked out the port as stars moved to new positions and smiled wryly, remembering the hours of watching and working he had done to do the same job badly.

Then the waiting began. The needles on the control board moved as the computer ran up the output of the atomic engines in preparation for the firing of the jets. Finger-chewing minutes passed until the computer decided that the correct moment had arrived. It did not inform them that it was time. The first that they knew was when the jets fired and a sudden, sideways thrust pushed at them.

"Well, that's it then," Don said. "How soon before we know if we are on the correct course, Dr. Ugalde?"

The mathematician frowned in thought. "I would say that it will be an hour at least before a meaningful base line can be established. We will make observations for Mars Central, and as soon as their computer has established our new orbit we will be informed."

"Telephone, Captain," Kurikka said, and Don switched on the instrument before him. Rama Kusum's worried face looked out at him.

"Could you come to the sick bay, sir? There is a patient here with a fever and, well, I don't know quite what to do."

"Any other symptoms?"

"Nothing I can put my finger on, just a generally sick feeling, upset stomach, you know."

"I certainly do—and there is nothing to worry about. There are any number of mild infections that start that way. Just hold on and I'll come right up to have a look."

It was almost a relief to have a medical matter to worry about, rather than the responsibility for the entire spaceship. He was a trained doctor and he knew that he could handle anything that occurred. Only in the operation of the ship did he have a feeling of futility.

"I'll be in the sick bay, Chief. Call me as soon as there are any reports."

He opened the door and was almost run down by Hansen, the air tender. He was hurrying and looked frightened.

"I'm sorry, sir," he said. "I was coming to see you. In private, if I could."

Don closed the door behind him and glanced both ways. The corridor was empty.

"Right here is fine. What is it?"

"The oxygen, Captain, the rate of production has fallen off again. We are way below the replacement rate, and right now people are breathing the stored oxygen in the atmosphere of the ship. I'm taking out the excess carbon dioxide all right, so there is no build-up of concentration of that. But the oxygen . . ."

"How long before the effect will be noticeable?"

"It's noticeable right now! If you were to run around you would be out of breath mighty quick. And soon, two or three days . . ."

"Yes?"

"People are going to start dying, sir."

10

"No localized pain, Mr. Preece?" Don asked. He touched the man's neck and his armpits. There was no swelling of the lymph nodes that would indicate a major infection.

"No, and if there were I would tell you quickly enough." Preece had a lean face and a hawk-like nose, and was obviously used to having his orders obeyed. "I paid a lot of money for this trip and it hasn't been much of a holiday so far. Meteors, miserable food, my luggage stolen. Now this. If you ran a clean ship I wouldn't have caught anything."

"All spaceships have to be hospital clean, to prevent the spread of disease from planet to planet." The man's temperature was over 100, but his pulse and breathing were normal. "The chances are that you brought this infection with you from Earth. After an incubation period it has made its presence known."

"What is it?" he sounded worried now.

"Nothing major, we can be sure of that. So far it's just a fever and nothing else. I'm going to ask you to stay here in the sick bay for a few days, mostly to protect the other passengers. We'll give you some drugs to knock out the bug and some antipyretics to bring the fever down. You don't have anything to be concerned about."

The phone rang while Don was filling the hypodermic, and he almost dropped it in his haste to answer.

"Captain here."

"We've done it!" It was Kurikka, his normal reserve cracked by the sudden change of events. "Mars reports that our orbit is now right on the button, or close enough so that a minor correction will take care of it. Since the reaction mass was so short they have put us into a capture orbit, instead of a normal braking orbit."

"What is the difference?"

"Normally we head toward the spot where Phobos Station will be, and brake until we match orbits. But we have no mass left for braking. So we are aimed at Mars. Not close enough to hit the atmosphere, but still close enough in so that we'll be captured by their gravity field and will swing back into an orbit around the planet."

"This is very good news, Chief. Give my thanks to everyone for helping us do the job the right way."

"Everything will be in the green now."

Don cut the connection and memory returned. Everything was not in the green. It wouldn't do them much good to arrive safely in an orbit around Mars if they were all dead of suffocation at the time.

He gave the injections and started up the stairs to C deck where air technology control was located. This entire deck was given up to the ship's operations and supplies, and rang like a tomb now. He passed empty storerooms—even their doors had been removed—and the places where surplus machinery had been ripped from the deck. Hansen was waiting for him.

"Here are the charts, sir," he said. "You can see for yourself."

Don looked at the pages and the rows of figures blurred as fatigue pulled at him. He handed them back.

"I would rather not see for myself. You're the specialist and I'm going to ask you to explain just what is going on here. What, basically, is causing the drop in oxygen level?

Hansen pointed at the apparatus on one wall. An illuminated inspection port showed an almost transparent, green liquid.

"It's the phytoplankton, you can see them there, in the port. They are one-celled plants that float in water. When they receive the carbon dioxide we breathe out in the ship they convert it back into oxygen. We lost too many of them when the water was lost during the accident. And a lot more died or mutated during the solar storm. There are not enough left to produce the amount of oxygen we need."

"Is there any chance of growing more?"

Hansen shook his head. "I'm doing my best to weed out the mutant strains and encourage cell division and growth. But it's too slow. There is plenty of nutrient to be added to the water, but the rate of division can't be accelerated."

"I can appreciate that." Don looked around at the other machinery in the large compartment. "What is the rest of this apparatus?"

"Mostly water processing, testing, microscopic analysis, automated monitor system, and that kind of thing. Over there is the raw air processing. Filters to take out contaminants, and the carbon dioxide reducer."

"Doesn't that help?"

"Some, but not enough. I have it going flat out now. It breaks the carbon dioxide back down into carbon and oxygen all right, but it was just designed to take up the slack in the main system. Sort of fill in when there is an excess of CO_2 for limited periods."

Don tried to prod his tired brain.

"We have stored oxygen. Won't that help?"

"Negative, sir. Only for a limited time. The total stored oxygen is less than enough for a twelve-hour period for everyone on the ship."

"Then what can we do?"

"I don't *know!*" Hansen said, and his face was white with fear. Don was sorry he had asked. The man was doing his assigned job well enough, but he could not cope with the bigger problem.

"Then don't worry about it, we'll come up with something."

Easy words to say—but what *could* they do? Where could they get more oxygen in the depths of interplanetary space? Think! He cudgeled his tired brain but the results were a complete blank. Yet he had the gnawing feeling that the answer was right before his eyes.

The only thing before his eyes were the tiny plants in their watery environment. They were doing their best, he knew that, yet the answer was there. But where . . . ?

Don laughed out loud.

"The answer *was* right in front of our eyes!" he said, and clapped the astonished air tender on the back. "Look in here —what do you see?"

"Why . . . the plankton, sir."

"Anything else?"

"No, nothing. Just them in the water. . . ."

"What was that last word?"

"Water."

"And what is water made of?"

Sudden comprehension brightened Hansen's face. "Hydrogen . . . and *oxygen!*"

"Absolutely correct. And we have all the power we need from the atomic generator. By feeding electricity into water, the two elements will be separated by the process of electrolysis. . . ."

"We bleed the hydrogen off into space—and use the oxygen. But, Captain, we need the water too. The plankton are still necessary."

"I wasn't thinking of depriving them. But I'm looking forward to more complaints from the passengers! All the ship's water is recycled—but we have far more than we need for survival. We'll determine the minimum amount needed and leave that much. The rest can be converted to oxygen. They may be dirty and a little thirsty—but at least they will be breathing!"

"What will we need for equipment?"

Don, feeling the drag of fatigue again, sat down wearily before he answered. He ticked off the points on his fingers.

"A container first, something like a bathtub. There's nothing complex about the reaction, and the container doesn't have to be sealed. We need direct current. A heavy cable from the generator will take care of that. Then we must have a weak solution of electrolyte to conduct the current. A simple salt or base dissolved in water."

"Table salt?"

"That's what we *don't* want! That is sodium chloride— which means we will be getting some chlorine mixed in with our oxygen and we positively do not need a poison gas like that. We need an alkaline salt. Do you have anything like that among your plant nutrients?"

Hansen pulled out his supply list and ran down it. "Will this do?" he asked. "Magnesium is essential for the production of chlorophyll, so we have a store of magnesium sulphate. . . ."

"Epsom salts! Couldn't be better. The only complication will be making some sort of container and piping for the cathode, the negative electrode in the solution. That's where the hydrogen will form. We'll draw that off and release it into space. The oxygen from the anode can just bubble off into the air." He made a quick sketch of the details and passed it over to the air tender.

"This should work fine, sir," Hansen said. "We can use that glass-lined settling tank there for a vessel. I'll clean it out and mix a weak solution of electrolyte. But I'm not sure about the wiring, or pumping out the oxygen."

"I'll get you some help. Chief Kurikka will know how to rig it, and if he doesn't he'll know who in the ship's crew will be able to do the job. Get him down here."

Kurikka brought Sparks, then called in Acting First Engineer Tyblewski. The cables from the now vanished frozen food lockers were located under the decks and torn out to bring in the necessary amount of current. While this was being done, a glass dome, formerly a viewport in the observatory, was put over the cathode, and piping hooked from it to a valve that connected with the vacuum outside the ship. This could be adjusted so that the hydrogen was drawn off, but not the watery electrolyte.

"Ready," Sparks announced finally.

"Well, let her go," Don said, so weary he could hardly sit up.

Kurikka threw the heavy-duty switch and Tyblewski slowly turned the handle on the rheostat. As current was fed to the electrode immersed in the bath, tiny bubbles began to form about it. Then, more and more, as the current was increased, large bubbles rose up and broke on the surface. Don leaned over and breathed deeply.

"Wonderful!" he said, as the pure oxygen cleared his head. "It looks like our problems are over once and for all."

He blinked, happily, in the oxygen rich atmosphere so close above the tub, and was only vaguely aware of a phone ringing, and the handpiece being passed over to him.

"Speaking," he said, then looked down to see the tiny image of Rama Kusum on the screen.

"Would you come to the sick bay, sir. There are four more cases of fever, just like the first. And the first one, I do not know what to do about him. He is in a coma and his pulse is very slow and I cannot awaken him!"

11

Don had dismissed Rama, told him to get some sleep, because he wanted to be alone with this problem. The four new cases of fever were in the larger ward, but the first case, Preece, was in the isolation room. Don stood by his bed, listening to the man's heavy, slow breathing and looking at the battery of recording instruments that had been hooked up to the patient's body. The situation was clear—but what did it mean?

Pulse, slow by steady. Heart, apparently normal. Temperature, 102 degrees and rising steadily despite the doses of antipyretics that were supposed to bring it down. The antibiotics, also, had apparently had no effect. What was the cause? A little earlier he had been priding himself that he could take care of any medical emergency that might arise. He wasn't doing too well with this one. And he was tired. . . .

Stifling a yawn, he went out into his office and carefully washed his hands and arms, then put them into the ultrasonic sterilizer. Rama had left a thermos of hot coffee and he poured himself a cup. While he sipped at it he tried to fit the facts into a meaningful pattern.

What were the facts—other than he had five patients hospitalized with a fever of unknown origin? The only specific symptom that Preece, the one with the most advanced case, presented was a peculiar twitching of his face and jaw. Very much like Colliver's symptom, though not as regular or strong. But this was *not* Colliver's symptom, which occurred only in the paralytic stage of poliomyelitis. There were no other polio symptoms and it could not possibly be that disease. Then what was it?

Like a dog worrying at an old bone, he kept returning to the thought that it was a disease that he had never heard of before. Which was certainly impossible. Diseases mutated or changed, or were very rare. But there were no *new* diseases. This must be one of the rare ones. He could waste days going through his library, so he had to narrow down the field a bit. Preece was his only lead. As the first victim there was a good chance that he was also the carrier. Don pulled the phone to him and dialed the purser's office.

"Jonquet, I need some information about a passenger."

"What do you require, sir? My records are quite near."

"I have a passenger here named Preece. I want to know where he comes from, and where he went before he boarded this ship. Any information at all that you have on him."

"One moment, sir. Will you hold on—or should I ring you back?"

"I'll be in my office, in the sick bay that is."

He hung up as Rama Kusum came in with a covered tray.

"I had dinner, Captain, and the thought occurred to me that perhaps you had not dined lately. So I took the liberty. . . ."

Don concentrated, but could not remember the last time he had eaten. But he was almost too tired to be hungry now.

"Thanks, but I doubt if I could eat. I saw some of those reconstituted dehydrated meals and I'm sure that they are nutritious. But they looked too much like damp sawdust. Not right now—"

He broke off as Rama put the tray down on the desk before him and uncovered it. A smoking steak lay on the plate, the succulent odor causing him to automatically lick at his lips. He started to reach for the silverware—then looked up in sudden anger.

"I ordered that all foodstuffs except the dehydrated meals be disposed of. I will not have favoritism or special privileges for anyone, myself included."

"Never, sir!" Rama backed away, hands raised against Don's anger. "It is a very simple story. Chief Kurikka discovered one of the cooks preparing this for himself. He had apparently hidden it for his own swinish use. The chief is a just man, but an angry one, and I tremble to tell you of the greedy cook's punishment. The least part of which was the careful preparation of this steak, but not the eating of same. It was the concerted agreement of all present that discarding it would be a waste. And that if anyone on the Big Joe were to have it, it would have to be you. There were no dissenting votes on that, sir. Please eat it before it gets cold."

Don was silent a moment, then he took up the silverware. His voice was halting when he spoke.

"That is the least I can do. Please . . . thank them for me. It's a wonderful steak."

He finished it all and was just washing it down with the last of the coffee when the phone rang. It was the purser calling back.

"The information you requested, Captain. Very simple. The man in question left Earth from the Chicago Lake Rocket Station, and he is also a resident of Greater Chicago. He had not been out of the city for at least a year before this flight. Is that the information you want, sir?"

"Yes, thank you, that's what I want." Don slowly dropped the receiver back into place.

Dead end. There were no exotic diseases in Greater Chicago.

"Is anything wrong?" Rama asked.

Don straightened up, aware that his worries were showing on his face.

"Just a false lead. I am trying to determine the nature of the disease that these people have. It's difficult. To be perfectly frank with you—I haven't the vaguest idea of what is wrong. Since you plan to be a doctor some day, Rama, you might as well find out now that doctors are human. Cut us and we bleed. We do not know everything. That is, any one of us does not know everything. That's why we have specialists. And I am now going to call on a specialist. You had better stay on duty here. I'll be in the control room if you need me."

Either the corridors were getting longer or he was getting tireder. He passed one of the passengers on the way, Mrs. Something-or-other, he should remember her name. He nodded in greeting as they passed, but she just turned away and sniffed audibly. He had to smile. He could almost read her thoughts: baggage-stealing, food-stealing, water-stealing, phony captain!

Kurikka was alone in the control room, arms folded over his chest, as he slumped in the astrogator's chair and looked at the dials and readouts before him. He might have been asleep, except Kurikka was not the kind of man who slept on duty. He unfolded his six-foot form and stood up at attention, even though Don told him not to.

"On course, Captain. Everything in the green. Report from air technology said that the oxygen rate is holding steady."

"At ease, Chief. Sit back down." He looked him over, noting the wrinkled uniform—the chief was usually immaculate—and the dark hollows under the man's eyes. "How long has it been since you had any bunk time?"

"I'm not quite sure, sir. But I feel fine. Not tired at all. Undoubtedly because I don't drink or smoke and am always in bed by nine."

"You're a liar!" Don said, and they both smiled. "Are we in voice contact with Mars yet?"

"Not yet. But Dr. Ugalde showed me how to program the computer to cut a tape for any messages. Just give it to me and I'll type it out."

"It's simple enough. Ask them to contact Earth and have the United Diagnostic Center in London stand by. I'm going to want a consultation. I'll send a list of the symptoms, but get that message out first. It may take some time for them to set up a link."

"Consultation, for sickness. This has something to do with those patients you have?"

"It certainly does. I'm going to tell you, as my second in command, but I don't want it passed on. The first case appears to be getting serious. As far as I can tell, they all have the same thing. And I haven't the slightest idea of what it is."

The chief turned silently to the computer keyboard and tapped in the message.

Don sat in the captain's chair and tried to organize his

thoughts. Disease, cure, symptoms, everything whirled and would not come together in any meaningful pattern. . . .

The voice did not disturb him, and only the steady shaking of his arm brought Don back to consciousness. He opened his gummy eyes to see the chief bending over him.

"The United Diagnostic Center is standing by," Kurikka said.

"How long have I been asleep?"

"About four hours, sir. I checked with the sick bay and you weren't needed there. So I let you sleep."

"You're probably right, Chief—I certainly needed it." He looked around. Sparks was adjusting the jury-rigged transmitter and a rating was making entries in the ship's log. "Now I want you to transcribe a message for me."

Don dictated all the symptoms of the mysterious disease, and all the medical data about his patients—every fact that he knew, even the passengers' names and addresses, so that their medical records on Earth could be consulted. Then he yawned and stretched as the coded tape was fitted into the transmitter.

"I'm going to wash up," he said. "There's plenty of time before we can expect an answer. And see if you can't have some coffee sent down."

Don felt better than he had at any time since the nightmare events had begun, following the collision with the meteorite. He had had some sleep and, for a change, there were no pressing emergencies. There was the trouble with the disease, but he could share the responsibility for that with others. Before this he had been alone—but now he had all the tremendous medical resources of Earth behind him. It was a lot like using an elephant gun to shoot a gnat, but it did give him a feeling of security.

Mars Central relayed one message from London asking for some more details, and Don supplied what information he could. Rama reported no change in any of the patients so Don could afford to relax—for the first time in how many days?—and sip his coffee. When the message finally came from the Diagnostic Center he was not at all prepared for it.

"Hello, Big Joe, this is Mars Central calling. I have a message for Dr. Chase, from the United Diagnostic Center in London. Message follows. 'We regret that there is no existing disease that matches the symptoms and details relayed to us. Please keep accurate records as this disease appears to be unique.' End of message."

Unique! Don was on his feet and the unbreakable glass cup was rolling across the deck, spilling a dark dribble of coffee.

There would be no help from the outside. He was alone with this problem, more alone than he had ever been before.

"That doesn't sound so good," Kurikka said. Don smiled grimly.

"Not so good is a great understatement. For some reason, they can't seem to pinpoint the fever that is giving us trouble."

"If it's a fever, that doesn't sound too bad. Another five, six days we'll be orbiting Mars and they can send up all the doctors you need to help out."

"That's fine, as long as it is *just* a fever. . . ."

Don cut off as the phone rang. Kurikka picked it up and listened for a moment before covering the mouthpiece.

"It's Rama in the sick bay," he said. "He wants you at once."

"Did he say why?"

Kurikka looked around at the other men on the bridge and reached a decision.

"Yes. He said that the patient, Preece, he's dead."

12

"There was nothing you could do, sir," Rama said.

"Perhaps. . . ." Don started to say, but could not finish. He knew that Rama was right. He turned away as Rama pulled the sheet up over the dead man's face.

They had tried everything. Transfusions, cooling bath, heart stimulation, drugs, everything. And nothing had worked. Preece had died, just died, his life turned off like the switching off of a light bulb. All of the powers of modern medicine could do nothing to reverse the process or restore him to life.

"I can tell you now," Rama said, in a low voice. "We have another two patients. I admitted them while you were working in here. Did London say what the disease is? What we can do to stop it?"

Don shook his head in a slow *no,* realizing that in the frantic rush to try to restore the patient's life he had never told Rama Kusum about the last message.

"They have no idea what it is either. We are all alone in this."

"But they *must* know," Rama insisted. He had an almost religious respect for the unlimited powers of medicine. "They know about all diseases, so they must know about this disease."

"They don't appear to know a thing about this one."

"That is impossible—unless it is a new disease."

"Which it appears to be. How Preece was infected before he boarded this ship has now become only of academic interest. Since there will be no help from the outside we shall have to stop it right here. So the first thing will be to prevent the spread of the infection. We will have to quarantine the sick bay, then make some arrangement to stop the spread to others. We must find out who the present patients may have contacted, then see if we cannot possibly separate them too."

"That will be very hard to do in a ship this size."

"Probably. And perhaps impossible. But we have to at least try. I'm going to the control room and I'll be back as soon as I can."

He phoned ahead and his officers were waiting when he came in—Sparks at the radio, Tyblewski from the engine room, the purser, and Kurikka. The chief must have received the message while he was shaving because one cheek was smooth while the other was covered with stiff bristles.

"At ease, sit down," Don ordered, and wondered how to tell them. Straight, it was the only way. They were trained spacemen and were not afraid to face facts.

"All of you here are volunteers—because I just volunteered for you. We have some cases of fever in the sick bay, and more coming in. And the first patient has just died. I can tell you, frankly, that no one even knows what the disease is. I am going to quarantine the sick bay and the bridge. I have been exposed to this disease, so I should quarantine myself in the sick bay alone. However, I am still in command of this ship. I don't really know how much risk of infection there is, but I am afraid that I must ask you all to stay on duty in the control room when I am here."

"There's nothing else to do, Captain. It couldn't be any other way," Kurikka said, speaking for all of them. "How is the quarantine going to work?"

"I want to isolate the sick bay. There are water taps there, and if we move in some boxes of dried rations it will be self-sufficient. Then I want to have all of the passengers transferred to the other side of the ship, as far away as possible. I know there will be complaints, but we should be used to them by now. Lastly, I want to set up a secondary area of quarantine for passengers who were exposed to any-one who is now down with the disease. Roommates, wives, friends. We don't know how the disease is spread, but if we do this quickly enough we may be in time to slow it down. Purser, do you have your passenger list with you?"

Jonquet nodded and tapped the folder beside him.

"Good, then let's go to work. I want the two lists as soon as is possible."

It was Chief Kurikka, the man who had helped build the *Johannes Kepler,* who noticed the relationship. He looked up suddenly from the control board while the names and com-partment numbers were being called out. He frowned, and his frown deepened as the numbers were written down. Un-noticed by the others he went to the chart cabinet and riffled through it. He produced a large blueprint and spread it out upon the table and studied it carefully. Only when he had verified his suspicion did he make it public.

"Captain, would you look at this, please?"

Don came over and stared at the blueprint, one of the cross sections of the spaceship.

"What about it?" he asked.

The chief tapped it with a broad finger, then produced a stub of red pencil. "These are the compartments that were penetrated by that meteorite. The ones that were open to space, then sealed and pressurized again." He drew a ring around each of them.

"Jonquet," he called out, "will you read me the compartment numbers of the patients now in sick bay."

As each number was read he tapped the compartment on the blueprint. Don looked on with growing disbelief. Only when the list was finished did he look up at the chief.

"Are you trying to suggest . . ."

"I'm not trying to suggest anything, sir," Kurikka said grimly. "Just pointing out a fact."

"But what kind of a fact is this? Every one of the patients now down with this fever is from a compartment that was holed. They had the good luck to be in other parts of the ship when the meteorite hit. But what can it mean? It has to be a coincidence."

"I don't believe much in coincidences, Captain. Not when so many people are involved. One, maybe two. But *all* of them?"

Don laughed. "It has to be a coincidence. Otherwise you are suggesting that there is some connection between the meteorite and his disease."

"You're suggesting it, sir. I'm just pointing out a fact."

"There just can't be a relationship!" Don paced back and forth, while the others looked on in silence. "All of the air was evacuated from those compartments. The temperature dropped. Then they were sealed and the air pumped back in.

But no one returned until the temperature, everything, had returned to normal. It's not a matter of just catching a cold, or anything like that." He stopped dead, suddenly, his eyes widening.

"No, it's an impossible thought," he insisted. "Chief, what was our position when we were hit?"

Kurikka pulled out another chart and pointed. "Roughly here, sir." Don looked and nodded.

"Between Earth and Mars, on the plane of the ecliptic, correct?" Kurikka agreed. "Then, one important question, what *else* is on this plane, between Earth and Mars?"

"Nothing."

"Don't be too quick to answer. What about the asteroids?"

Kurikka smiled and tapped the chart again. "Out here, Captain, way out between Mars and Jupiter, that's where the asteroids are."

"If I remember my astronomy, aren't there some asteroids, like Apollo and Eros, whose orbits not only come inside the orbit of Mars, but inside the orbit of *Earth* as well?"

The smile faded from Kurikka's face. "That's true, I had forgotten about them."

"Then—and this is the important question—if major asteroids are in this area, isn't it possible that we were struck by a smaller fragment of asteroid, one of the pieces of space rock that make up the asteroid belt?"

"Very possible, sir. A very good chance that's what it was. But what is the importance of this?"

"The importance is that the best theory of the origin of the asteroids that we have states that they are the debris of another planet that once existed in orbit between Mars and Jupiter. And the chunk that hit us was from this planet."

There were baffled looks on all sides, but Jonquet was the first to understand where the train of supposition was heading.

"*Mon dieu!*" he breathed, and his face was suddenly pale. "Are you suggesting that this disease, this fever, came from the meteorite? That this is a disease from a planet that was destroyed millions of years ago?"

"I'm suggesting just that. The idea is not as preposterous as it sounds. You must realize that I have given every test imaginable to the fever victims, and have made blood examinations, stool cultures, sputum and urinanalysis. This ship is equipped with a small electron microscope, and if there were any microorganisms there I would have found them. But you can't see a virus with this microscope. I am certain that this is a virus infection that we are battling, but I have no idea which virus it is. Now there are perhaps some facts about viruses that you may not know. They are the smallest forms of life, right on the borderline between living and inanimate matter. In fact some scientists don't believe that they are alive at all. They have been constructed in laboratories from neutral chemicals, and the artificial forms were proven to be identical with the natural ones. Some of them, when dried, appear to be very stable and can be revitalized after many years in this state. We know that they remain unchanged for hundreds of years—so perhaps they can exist in this neutral condition for thousands, even millions of years.

"No wonder the disease could not be identified. It *is* a new one on Earth. Though it may have existed for a far longer time than we care to imagine. If this supposition is true then we are the victims of a plague from another world. A disease against which our bodies have no defense at all, against which our medicines are totally ineffective."

Jonquet's whispered words were loud in the silence that followed.

"Then—we are all dead men. . . ."

"No!" Don shouted, trying to break the aura of despair that filled the control room. "This may give us a chance. I have enough equipment aboard to construct a RNA analyzer and duplicator. I haven't considered it before this because it is necessary to have only a single virus to duplicate, while there are many different kinds in our bloodstreams and those of the victims of the fever. I had no way of separating out the infectious strain, because that is a long and complicated laboratory procedure. But I do have a chance now to prepare a viricidal agent. Chief, don't I remember your telling me something about the meteorite that hit us still being lodged somewhere in the ship?"

"Yes, here in the unpressurized hold, in the center of the ship." He pointed to the spot on the blueprint. "In the center of the wheel here are the cargo holds that are open to space, bulk cargo and containers and that kind of thing. It's in there somewheres."

"Could we find it?"

"Why yes, I guess so. But why . . . ?"

"To get samples of this virus in its dried state. If particles that were brushed off as this thing went through the ship could reconstitute themselves and cause the disease, I see no reason why I cannot do the same in the laboratory. If I can, there is a good chance that I can manufacture a cure for the disease. It's a long shot, but I don't see any other possibilities of stopping the spread."

"Sounds good to me," Kurikka said. "I'll get a spacesuit and track that thing. I'll bring it back if it's still there."

"Get two suits—because I'm going with you. I want to be

there when we find it and examine it. I want to make sure it doesn't cause any more trouble when we bring it in."

"You're the captain, you shouldn't risk—"

"It's more important that I be a doctor now. The ship's running smoothly enough. But I'm the only person who can do anything with this virus material—if it exists. I'll be coming with you, Chief."

The door had opened while they were talking, but no one had noticed it. They wheeled about, now, when the voice spoke.

"No one is going anywhere."

General Briggs stood in the doorway with a revolver in his hand. Doyle and two other men pushed in behind him, carrying lengths of metal.

"I am now in charge of this ship, *doctor,* and you will return to the sick bay where you belong. You made a mess of things after you assumed command, and I assure you that all the passengers feel the same as I do. They agree that a man who is used to command, myself, should act as captain. Now proceed to your duties—and forget this wild plan and any other insane ideas that may be hatching in your head.

"You are an ordinary doctor again, and I am in command of the *Johannes Kepler.*"

13

In the shocked silence that followed this announcement the general and his followers pushed into the control room. It was Chief Kurikka who reacted first, stepping forward, ignoring the gun that swung to cover him.

"What you are attempting is piracy," he said, in a stern voice, used to command. "By the ruling of the World Convention piracy in space is as vicious a crime as piracy on the high seas, and will be punished even more sternly. A life sentence is the minimum penalty. You will not escape this. Lay down your weapons now, before you go too far. I'll take that revolver."

It was almost successful. Some of the men behind Briggs lowered their improvised clubs and looked at each other worriedly. Kurikka strode forward determinedly, his hand out for the gun. The general moved back before him.

"If you try to take this gun away I shall be forced to shoot you," he said, no less positive than the chief.

"Then you will face a charge of murder as well as piracy. You will spend the rest of your life in jail. Hand it over!"

Briggs stepped back again. "Take him out, Doyle," he ordered, without turning his head.

Doyle swung his bar, catching the chief on the shoulder, knocking him to the deck.

"We are determined men," Briggs said. "We will not be stopped."

The resistance was over. The chief was on the deck, trying to rise. More armed passengers came in from the corridor.

"You won't get away with it," Don said. "You know nothing about the operation and navigation of this ship. And you can't count on the crew for any help."

Briggs' mouth curved into a cold smile. "On the contrary, we have at least one man who knows a good deal about the operation of this vessel. The crewmen off duty will be locked up, and there will be at least two guards with every one on duty. They will not refuse to work, since that would endanger their own lives as well as ours. There will be no trouble, Doctor. Particularly with my first mate in command. You have met Dr. Ugalde?"

Ugalde pushed through, holding a well-sharpened kitchen knife. He nodded curtly and went to sit in the captain's chair. Don was shocked, he had never thought that the Mexican mathematician would betray them. A sense of defeat overwhelmed him: he turned back to the general.

"All right, Briggs, you have control of the ship for whatever good it will do you. . . ."

"It will get us to Mars safely."

"It will get you a certain jail term," Kurikka said, struggling to his feet. "Smuggling a weapon aboard a spaceship is a serious crime."

"I am always armed, despite any petty regulations."

"I don't care about your gun or even your stupid piracy,"

Don called out angrily. "But I care about the lives of everyone aboard. I must get that meteorite out. . . ."

"No. Get to your patients, Doctor. I'll not tell you again."

"You don't understand. I cannot cure them or even treat them. But if we can examine the meteorite I may be able to find a—"

"Take him out," Briggs ordered, waving two men forward. "I heard just enough of this harebrained theory to know that it is as mad as your other schemes. My first act when we reach Mars will be to propose that you be investigated by a lunacy commission. In the meantime—try to be a doctor, if you are still able to."

Numbed by defeat, Don did not resist as two burly passengers pushed him into the corridor. They followed behind warily as he went up to the sick bay, then stayed on guard outside when he went in.

"What has happened?" Rama asked, frightened at the look on Don's face. He was even more frightened after Don had explained what had happened.

"We must resist, fight! You have saved all their lives and this is your reward. That such evil should exist in the world!" He began to throw open the cabinets, searching for the largest scalpels. Don tried to quiet him.

"That's not the way. These men are armed and ready. And they are frightened or they would never have allowed Briggs to bring them to this open revolt. In fact it matters very little who is in command of the ship, as long as we get to Mars safely. What *does* matter is that I think I have found a way to manufacture a cure for this disease— but Briggs won't let me. We must do something!"

They could do nothing. The guards outside were changed at regular intervals and remained alert. For the first few hours the telephones would not work. The general had disconnected them while taking over the ship. Once he was securely in control he must have felt sure of his position, because the phone service was restored. Don tried calling the engine room, but one of Briggs' men answered the phone. The same thing happened when he tried air technology, and all of the other places where crewmen were on duty. The crew members were being kept apart from each other, and appeared to be outnumbered at least two to one by their captors when they were on duty. The ship could not be retaken.

With a feeling of intense despair Don tried to aid his patients. There were fourteen of them now, and the first ones to be stricken were sinking fast. He tried every combination of antibiotics and medicines in the vain hope that he might accidentally stumble onto a cure. Nothing worked.

Exhausted by strain and fatigue, he finally lay down, fully dressed, and tried to sleep. It was the middle of the ship's night. Though the spacer was in continuous day, with the sun shining all of the time, a regular cycle of day and night was followed. Not only did this permit the meals and social affairs to occur at set times, but it was essential for the health of the people aboard. The human body has a circadian rhythm, regular times for waking and sleeping, that causes difficulties if upset. Therefore the ship slept at "night" and only the crewmen on duty were normally awake at this time.

Don slept, but was awakened at 0400 hours, shiptime, by the repeated ringing of the telephone. He fumbled for it and the screen lit up with the image of Doyle, the general's secretary.

"Tell the guards to come in," he ordered. "I want to talk to them."

Don's first thought was to slam the phone down. Let them carry their own messages—he didn't want to help them! But there was nothing to be gained by this, as much as he would enjoy doing it, so he went to the door. The guards were suspicious and one of them watched Don closely while the other answered the phone. He listened, then hung up.

"They want the doctor in the control room," he said. "I'm to bring him down while you stay here."

"Did they say why?" the other man asked.

"Someone is sick. Grab your little black bag, Doc, and let's go."

Don washed the sleep from his eyes and took an emergency kit from the locker. Another case of fever? He wondered who it was and, knowing the feeling was most unprofessional, he hoped that it was the general. The rebellion would undoubtedly fall apart if he were out of the way. He started for the control room with the guard following close behind.

A guard outside nodded as they came up, then opened the door for them. The first thing Don saw when they entered was Sparks lying on the deck. His eyes were closed and he moaned and clutched at his stomach. Dr. Ugalde was in the captain's chair while Doyle was on the other side of the room holding the gun.

"Take care of him," Doyle ordered. "He's sick. He just folded up and collapsed. We need him on the radio."

"I touched his head and it was most warm," Ugalde said.

This was not the way the fever usually began, but anything was possible with a new disease. Don knelt by Sparks and snapped open his case. As he took out the recording telltale he laid the back of his hand against the man's forehead. His skin was cool, his temperature perfectly normal.

Before Don could say anything Sparks opened his eyes— then closed one again in a long, deliberate wink.

At this same moment the door to the corridor opened and he recognized Kurikka's voice.

"Drop that gun, Doyle, and no one will get hurt."

Don spun about and saw that the scene had changed dramatically. Kurikka stood in the open doorway, pushing the disarmed hall guard before him. He held a large automatic pistol which he leveled steadily at Doyle. Dr. Ugalde now stood behind the other guard and had the point of his knife pressed into the side of the man's neck.

"Drop the weapon," Ugalde snarled, in a voice quite different from his normal one, "or I will drive this knife deep into your throat and kill you instantly."

The bar clanged to the deck.

Doyle hesitated, confused, looking from one to the other of them—then brought up his pistol.

Kurikka's gun fired just once and Doyle howled in pain. His pistol dropped from his fingers and he clutched at his arm. Slow blood oozed between his fingers.

Sparks rose to his feet and cheered, then picked up the fallen gun. Don was dazed.

"Kurikka," he asked, "how did you manage it?"

The chief smiled and lowered his automatic. "Thank Dr. Ugalde. He arranged the whole thing and masterminded the plot."

Ugalde beamed with pleasure and bowed slightly when they all looked toward him.

"There is much precedent, in my country, for this sort of thing. The misguided General Briggs approached me for aid, knowing of the revolutionary background of my ancestors. I accepted at once, because he had neglected to remember the *counter-revolutionary* history of my land. It is far easier to work from inside an evil organization. I joined, entered his highest councils, then waited until the night. It must always be considered that movements are easier to destroy early, before they have become established. At this time, if you will excuse my saying so, it was just a matter of waiting for an opportunity. As soon as the general retired, and left his creature, Doyle, with the gun, I knew we must strike. A telephone call to Chief Kurikka alerted him for his part, and he was kind enough to inform me that he knew where a weapon was concealed in the captain's cabin. The information is not commonly known, but there is always a gun aboard every craft for emergencies, madmen, and the like. A most foresighted conception. Then, one, two, three, Sparks collapses on cue, you are sent for, Chief Kurikka arrives, and the matter is over. . . ."

"Not quite. You still have to deal with me."

General Briggs stood in the door, his face white with anger. He stepped into the room, looking about him coldly.

"You will not be able to get away with this pathetic little plot," he said. "I was informed as soon as the doctor left the sick bay. There was always a chance that this madman, in desperation, might attempt to regain the ship. That is not to be."

He pointed back to the door where a number of men armed with clubs and bludgeons waited.

"Now lay down your weapons and there will be no violence." Briggs even smiled, condescendingly. "Do it at once and there will be no reprisals or bloodshed. Now—hand over that gun!"

He raised his hand and started toward Kurikka. The chief slowly lifted his weapon and centered it between the general's eyes.

"Come any closer and you are dead."

The general stopped.

"I want to avoid bloodshed," he said. "This is your last chance to surrender. You do not have enough bullets in that gun to kill us all—and we are desperate men."

There was a paralyzing silence in the control room as the two men faced each other. No one moved.

"It won't do, Briggs," Don said, his voice stern with authority. "You're a fake and you know it. A bitter, evil little man, and a bungling pirate as well. No one is going to die for you. I am the captain of this ship, and I promise leniency to you men if you drop your weapons at once. . . ."

"Don't listen to him!" Briggs shouted, his voice cracking with rage, his face flushed red. "Attack! Get them!"

But the spell had been broken by Don's words, and the armed men wavered. They would fight for their lives if they thought they had something to win. But they could not face the black eye of certain death in the muzzle of the chief's unwavering automatic. They moved restlessly, looking at each other—but they did not advance.

"Cowards!" General Briggs screeched. He bent and grabbed up the steel bar that the guard had dropped. "Not a man among you. Follow me—this one won't shoot, kill in cold blood. He's a bigger coward than all of you." He started forward.

"I wouldn't if I were you," Kurikka said. Then he cocked the heavy hammer and the clack was loud in the silence. The gun was steady.

"You won't shoot," Briggs sneered, raising his weapon.

"Anyone else I would, but not you," the chief said, lowering the gun. "I want to see you on trial."

Shouting victoriously, the general swung the bar at the chief's head.

For a big man the chief moved as swiftly as a cat. He stepped forward a single pace and blocked the rush of the blow with his upraised arm—letting the general's forearm strike against the metal pistol butt. There was a gasp of agony and the bar slipped from Briggs' paralyzed fingers. Pivoting on his toes, Kurikka brought his left fist up in a short, wicked jab to the other man's midriff.

The general folded, curled up, falling down and out upon the deck. Kurikka ignored him and pointed the weapon at the men in the doorway.

"I will now shoot any man who does not drop his weapon. *Drop it!*"

There was no doubt that he meant it. The bars and clubs clanged to the floor and the piracy was over. Kurikka looked down at the still form of the general and his bleak face broke into a humorless smile.

"You have no idea what pleasure that gave me," he said.

Don went to Doyle, who had collapsed, green-faced, in his chair, and examined the neat bullet hole in his forearm.

"National Pistol Champion," Kurikka said. "I never miss."

Don shook antibiotic powder on the wound and snapped open a pressure bandage. He looked up abruptly when his fingers touched Doyle's skin: he pushed a telltale against the arm.

"Doyle has it," he said. "A temperature of 103."

"I am not surprised," Dr. Ugalde said. "I did not wish to mention it earlier, it would just have caused confusion, but I am forced to admit that my own temperature has been above normal for the past few hours, and that I am feeling distinct pains of an uncomfortable sort."

"Kurikka," Don said, "we have to find that meteorite, as quickly as we can. We've run out of time."

They looked at each other, and each man saw his own cold fear reflected in the other's eyes.

14

"Another jury-rig," Sparks said. "Do you think it will do the job?"

"It pretty well has to, doesn't it?" Don asked, trying not to be depressed as he looked at the collection of plundered equipment that sprawled across the tiny bench in the sick bay laboratory. "The theory is right, and we checked it out with the hospital at Mars Central. They have built a duplicate of this thing, using the same parts, and it worked fine on the test run. If we follow their instructions, we should be able to run duplication on any RNA we find, and prepare a viricidal agent." If we find any, he added silently to himself.

All of the hectic work of the past ten hours would be useless if there were no meteorite there. Or if the theory were wrong, and the chunk of space rock had nothing to do with the disease. There were too many ifs. . . .

But it was the only chance they had. He pushed one leg into the spacesuit as Kurikka came in. He was wearing his suit, with the helmet hanging, and he carried a steel canister.

"I hope it will be big enough," he said.

"It has to be. It is bigger than the entrance hole the meteorite made, so whatever we find should fit into it. How does it work?"

Kurikka flipped up the flat metal lid that was hinged at the side of the container. "Simple enough. We put the meteorite in, then coat the inside of the lid with di-epoxy glue. This stuff works in a vacuum, anyplace. Seals airtight in about two minutes. You'll have to cut the end off to get at it, but that's no problem."

"Nothing will be a problem—once we find the meteorite." He sealed the spacesuit and reached for his helmet. "Let's go."

"How many sick now?" Kurikka asked.

"I stopped counting at ninety. Over half the people aboard. Three more dead."

He led the way, in silence, to the midpipe elevator. The drive wheels whined as it rose up toward the center of rotation of the ship. They became lighter and lighter until, when the elevator stopped, they floated weightless out of the door. Don followed behind, moving much slower than the chief, who was long used to null-G and drifted easily with an occasional touch on the guide rods. He had the hold airlock open when Don came up.

"We're entering the hold as close to the point of impact as we can get. We welded a patch on the floor plates of C deck about thirty feet from here. But we never entered the hold. We should be able to follow the path of the meteorite from the inside. But I have no idea how deep it penetrated. We only know that it didn't come out again."

"Inside the ship. But if it went out through the side, instead

of going through the decks again, is there any way that you would know that?"

"No," Kurikka said, grimly. "We can only hope that it didn't. Seal up, I'm starting the cycling."

They snapped their faceplates shut and waited in silence as the door closed and the air was pumped from the lock. When it was gone the green light flashed on and the other door opened automatically. They floated out into the darkness of the immense hold.

It was a nightmare world of light and shadow, and Don was disoriented and lost before they had moved more than a few feet from the airlock. In the airless hold the patches of darkness could be either shadow—or solid—there was no way of telling without touching the spot or flashing a light on it. They had lights built into their helmets, but Don found his difficult to use. He clutched to a steel brace and tried to steady himself. The chief floated up, his light sweeping a path before him. His voice rattled in Don's earphones.

"It's difficult at first, but you'll get the hang of it."

"There's no up or down—and when I try to move I get dizzy, disoriented."

"You're not the only one, sir. It always hits like this first time out. The thing to do is to fix your attention on one thing and try to ignore everything else. Now I'll go ahead, slowly, and you stay behind me. Keep looking square at me, eyes front, and that will keep your light focused on my back. If you want to look at something don't turn your eyes, but your whole head. That way you will have light wherever you look. Ready?"

"Ready as I'll ever be. Push off."

Kurikka pulled himself up a series of handholds along a beam. The space was tight, with great containers on both sides, looming shapes in the darkness. He reached a cross beam and angled out along it. There was a solid surface above his head and he trained his light up onto it.

"Look there," he said, pointing to a torn opening in the metal that was sealed with a shining plate on the other side. "Here's where it came through. That's the patch we put on the deck."

They turned their heads and the circles of light from their beams crossed and met on the surface of an aluminum container a few feet away. The black disk of an opening was punched into its surface.

"Is that it?" Don asked.

"Right. But before we tear into the container let's make sure that it's still inside. Stay here, I can work faster alone. I want to examine the skin of this thing."

The chief was right, it did not take long. Don flashed his light into the hole, but there was only darkness inside.

"I've found the exit hole," the chief's voice said in his earphones. "I'll take you to it."

The meteorite had emerged from the container and plunged into a bale nearby, one of many secured by a tight net of plastic strands.

"Clothing," the chief said, reading the label. "This is good luck. The layers inside will have slowed and stopped the thing, maybe even caught it. Use your knife, cut the net and we'll pull the bale out."

Cutting the plastic was easy enough, but extracting the bale, tightly wedged in by the others, proved impossible.

"We'll have to cut them all free," Kurikka said, slashing at the strands, "then shove them apart."

The bales surged and pushed against each other as the strain was released, moving with a life of their own. Soon there were bales floating all around them, bumping into them, getting in their way. With the pressure relieved, they grabbed the one they wanted and managed to heave it free. Kurikka turned it end for end and threw his light on it.

There was an exit hole in it.

"The next one. The meteorite is still further on," he said.

Floating bales filled the space around them, jammed against them when they tried to move. The second layer was still wedged tightly together.

"We'll never get these free," Don said.

"Maybe we won't have to—look!" He flashed his light into the opening and, deep down it lit up a roughened surface. "It's inside this one!"

With a quick slash of his knife he cut open the bale and heavy clothing drifted out. They rooted like mice in grain, hurling the clothing aside, stuffing it behind them, digging deeper and deeper until they came to it.

"That's it," Don said. He was exhausted and empty of any emotion.

It looked so commonplace. A chunk of dirty rock. He pried at it with his knife and it floated free, turning as it rose. When it rotated the other side came into view.

This side of the meteorite was hollowed out, and lined with whitish crystals.

"The can, quick!" Don said, pulling back. "And don't touch it with your gloves."

"Those crystals—are they what you want?" the chief asked, prodding the rock with his knife tip so that it floated into the container he was holding.

"I think so. I hope so." Don was soaked with sweat and his head hurt. "Seal it up."

With slow precision the chief took out the tube of di-epoxy

and squeezed a circle of it onto the lid, then flipped it shut. He pushed down hard to seal it, and made sure it was closed all the way around.

"In two minutes it will be harder than steel," he said.

"Good. Let's leave the knives here, they must be contaminated. And be careful taking off your suit, since we have surely brushed against material that is already contaminated."

"Right. Follow me back, this thing will be sealed before we reach the lock." He plowed away through the floating bales and clothing with Don staying close behind.

"What would a dried virus look like?" the chief asked, when they were in the lock and the air was being let back in.

"I have no idea, it could look like anything. These crystals perhaps." He wiped his glove across his helmet to remove the water film that condensed there as air rushed in. "When can we open our suits?"

"Not before the green light comes on. We'll do it outside of the airlock. The metal in here is chilled now, it can give you a bad burn."

When the door opened they floated out into the midpipe. Don put out his hand.

"Let me have the container," he said. "Then move away and take off your suit—without touching the outside. I'll pull on it if you need help. Then get out of here, back to the control room. I'll follow as soon as you are clear."

Kurikka protested. "You'll need help getting out of your suit. . . ."

"No I won't. I'm not concerned about contamination. I'm enough of a doctor to recognize the symptoms.

"I don't have to worry about catching the fever—because I already have it."

15

They had hit the fifty percent mark a day earlier, when the uninfected people had to quarantine out the ill ones. Now, four out of five people aboard the great ship were down with the fever.

Mars was two days away. Rockets were waiting, with volunteer nurses and doctors standing by. No one would be permitted to leave the *Johannes Kepler*. It was a plague ship—and would be kept quarantined that way until—if and when—a cure for the fever was found. Food, drugs, equipment, anything could be put aboard. Nothing could come out.

There were now twenty-two dead.

Don took another pain pill and blotted the sweat from his face with a damp towel. He was taking far more of the pills than were safe, he knew that, but he could not collapse. Not now. The equipment before him blurred and he blinked his eyes back into focus, then made an adjustment on the glass petcock that slowed the flow of reaction agent to a steady drip.

"Let me do that, Doctor," Rama said.

"You should not be in here, you don't have it yet."

"That is of no importance, sir. I am the only one who can aid you in any way and you must permit it. What is the condition of the duplication process now?"

"I don't know. I'm not sure if I am even doing anything, or if there even is a virus in this solution. We have no animals—other than ourselves—to test it on. But I dissolved those crystals in nutrient solution, different solutions at different temperatures. I filtered them, recombined them, and I put the resulting liquid through this apparatus. It may be clear water for all I know. . . ." His voice rasped and he coughed, then dabbed at his forehead again. "How is the situation in control?"

"I have just talked to them. Chief Kurikka is there, with Computerman Boyd. Neither of them is sick yet, so they are optimistic that they can bring the ship in. I unhappily report that Dr. Ugalde is in a coma, so can no longer aid. But Mars Control says that they can work through our computer and direct the final maneuvers even if no one is left in control. The remaining mass will be used to put us into as low an orbit as is possible."

The timer buzzed and Don started across the room to the ultracentrifuge. Suddenly, with no warning at all, he sprawled full length on the deck. His legs had simply given way. Rama put his arms around him and helped him to a chair.

"I'll be all right in a moment, Rama. Switch off the centrifuge, will you."

The shrill whine changed to a deepening moan as the rotating machine slowed to a stop.

"With some luck," Don said, levering himself to his feet, holding onto the back of the chair, "this could be it. This is the result of the first extraction. The viricidal agent."

"Shall we take it out, use it at once?" Rama asked excitedly.

Don shook his head *no*. "In a moment. First help me with the soup from these other jars." He held up the flask and looked at the murky fluid slopping about inside. "There are more of the crystals here in nutrient solution. I put them up at the same time as the ones I used for the first run. If there was nothing in the first solution, the viruses may not have been reconstituted yet, we may find it in here. We're working in the dark."

With careful precision he made the adjustments, poured in the liquid, and began the second run of the RNA duplication apparatus. Only then did he turn to the centrifuge and flip the lid open. He took out one of the vials and held it to the light. There was a brownish deposit on the bottom, with a clear liquid above.

"Bring me a syringe with a 20 gauge needle."

Inserting the point, he drew back his thumb and filled the cylinder.

"Take this," he said, handing it to Rama. "Inject the worst cases."

"The dosage?"

"I don't know—this stuff is concentrated—3.5 cc's I guess, at least that much. Intravenously. Worst cases first, then all the others. There is enough for everyone in the centrifuge. I have to watch the second run."

A buzzer. Temperature 110°. Filtrate. Careful, there's no more of this if you spill it. It would be easier if the hands didn't shake so. But the hands shake, so brace them. Pour it. Don't spill it.

A buzzer. What now? What came next? Cold water on the face, head under the faucet, that always helps. Is that me in the mirror? Haven't been shaving lately, have you, Doc? Frighten the patients with a face like that. Now, what comes next?

Lying on the floor, the salty taste of blood in the mouth. The sting of something on the cheek, a face above.

"Rama . . . ?"

"You fell, sir. A minor cut. I am dressing the wound. . . ."

Fear!

"The apparatus? Did I break any?"

"No, you must have felt it coming. You pushed yourself away, fell backwards. I heard the buzzer and it would not stop. What is next to be done?"

"Help me up and I'll show you."

Hard to think. The gray fog in his head was now before his eyes. It was very difficult to see through. It was very difficult to think. The patients?

"How long since the injections?"

"Over eight hours, sir. I gave you yours when—"

"How are they?"

There was a long silence and Don could make out Rama's face only as a blur: he finally answered.

"No change, no change at all. Two deaths. The Chief Kurikka fell ill in the control room and has been brought in."

"Is it all a waste? Are we all dead?" Don spoke hoarsely, to himself. "Will it all end like this? There can be no other answer."

It was time to give in, to collapse, to die. But he would not. With an effort of will, will alone because his body was failing him, he straightened up. His eyes could see, they *had* to see. He rubbed them with his knuckles, angrily, until he could feel the pain of the pressure even through the haze of drugs that enveloped him. Tears streamed down his cheeks and he could see, dimly, again. He stumbled to the bench.

"Turn off the buzzer. Here. Decant these, into those test tubes. Cool them. Then into the centrifuge. Four minutes spin. Then use."

"That will be the final solution, the cure?"

Don thought he was smiling, but his lips were curled back, like those of a horse in pain, his teeth showing widely. Speaking took immense effort.

"That will be a transparent liquid. Looking exactly like distilled water. It may be only distilled water. We have . . . we have . . ."

Blackness, and he was falling, and it was the end.

16

There were two mountains of blackness in a universe of darkness each as big as a world itself. Yet they moved, slowly, this way and that, the motion hard to see amidst the driving midnight streamers that blew past. And they talked, unknown words in an unknown tongue, nothing that could be of interest. Mountains, murmuring, rocking with the eternal motion of mountains. . . .

But the words could make sense. What else are words for?

". . . can begin . . ."

". . . or . . ."

". . . it over . . ."

Fragments, disconnected, words. From mountains? No, not mountains, presences. And they were speaking.

For a long time, measureless, Don held onto this idea and worried at it. It would drift away, and he would forget about it, but the voices were still there and they must mean something.

Sometime during this period he realized that his eyes were closed. His memory was nothing but a patch of gray and his body was numb and somehow disconnected from his thoughts. The eyes were the first part, because the mountains were people, pushing him toward consciousness and he wanted to see who they were. With infinite labor he opened his eyes and looked at the blurred presence. A white shape.

"Doctor, his eyes are open."

The voice helped him to focus and when he did a girl's face, a white nurse's uniform, swam into view. He had never seen her before. How could there be someone on the ship he had never seen before? And the other figure, white dressed too, a doctor, another doctor, also someone he had never seen before. He looked up at them and the doctor had to speak the obvious to him, his thoughts were that numb. Had to tell him what his eyes saw and what he could not understand.

"You are not well, but you are alive. You will recover. I want you to think about that while you go back to sleep."

Like a child obeying a command he closed his eyes and drifted into a dreamless sleep.

The next time he awoke he was rational. Sick, exhausted, limp as a wet rag and unable to move. But rational. And the strange faces were not there this time, but instead the familiar dark features of Rama Kusum swam over the foot of the bed. His eyes were wide and he raised both hands with excitement.

"Chief," he called out, "Chief Kurikka—come at once! He is awake!"

There were heavy footsteps and Kurikka appeared at his side, smiling.

"We made it, Captain. You pulled us through."

Those were the words he wanted to hear. The chief had

known how he felt. They had made it. Did anything else count? Don tried to talk but his voice cracked and he started to cough. Rama rushed him a glass of water and held the straw to his lips. It was cool and it felt good going down. This time he succeeded.

"What happened. Tell me everything." His voice was only a hoarse whisper: he could speak no louder.

"It was a close one, Captain, that's for certain." Rama nodded solemn agreement to the chief's words.

"Rama called me when you collapsed, I was right there in the sick bay. I wasn't feeling so good myself. Everyone in the ship had it by that time. We laid you on the bunk and Rama showed me the second solution you were running through the equipment. When it came out of the centrifuge he gave you the first shot, then I helped him with the patients in the sick bay. There was one of them dead, I remember that clearly, because he was the last one who died. It was that Doyle, believe it or not, so he won't be standing in the dock next to the general when that day comes."

"The general . . . ?"

"Alive and well," Kurikka smiled coldly. "Be in fine shape for the trial. But that's not the important part, not now. It was you, just like night and day, Captain. Unbelievable if we hadn't seen it with our own eyes. We emptied those hypos and came back for more, and Rama here took a look in at you and I heard him gasp. I moved fast then, I can tell you."

"Minutes," Rama said, "just minutes. And the fever was gone and you were lying quiet, even snoring in natural sleep. The ravages of the disease were not gone that instantly, to be sure, but the fever instantly stopped.

"The second batch of juice that you cooked up was it.

The people who had just been hit by the bug almost climbed out of bed after the injections. Stopped it dead. We injected everyone in the ship, and had the engine room and control room manned next day when we went into orbit. They didn't have to bring us in, sir, the Big Joe did it herself."

"You are tiring him," a new voice said. "You will have to leave."

Don looked at the doctor in the doorway and shook his head on the pillows, smiling. "This is better than medicine, Doctor."

"I'm sure of it. But I think it is enough for the moment. After you have slept they can come back."

When they had gone the doctor took a hypodermic from the bedside table. When Don turned to look he saw, for the first time, that he wasn't in his own bunk. The bed was bigger, as was the room. It was the captain's quarters he realized, when he saw the large photo of the *Johannes Kepler* on the wall, and the repeating instruments from the control room.

"Just a few questions before I go to sleep," he said, and the doctor nodded agreement.

"My patients, how are they?"

"All far better than you are, and still aboard. Your miracle cure worked all right, but the ship is still quarantined until we can make the proper analysis to be absolutely sure. You're the worst of the lot. You drugged yourself and overloaded your system and, to be very frank, it was touch and go for a while there."

"But I had to—didn't I?"

The doctor opened his mouth, but did not answer. He smiled. "Yes, I imagine you did have to. I'm glad you were aboard, because I doubt very much if I could have done it. Now, the shot."

"A moment, please. About the so-called mutiny. What do the authorities mean to do with the people? You must realize the situation, that there was provocation. . . ."

"They know that, and I doubt if any of them other than General Briggs will stand trial. That is my unofficial opinion, but I know that the people on the top feel the same way. It *was* piracy. You are a ship's officer and were in command of this ship. You still are for that matter, since a new commander has not been appointed yet. So—I don't know whether to call you doctor or captain—but in either case you are going to sleep now."

Don did go to sleep, smiling.

The following morning after he had eaten, the nurse rubbed on depilatory cream to remove his whiskers and propped him up with extra pillows.

"What's this for?" he asked, suspiciously.

"You're having guests. You have to look your best."

"So it's guests now. I thought I was too sick for visitors? At least that's what you have been telling me. While I have been telling you . . ."

"A doctor who prescribes for himself has a fool for a patient," she said, and flounced out. Don smiled after her.

"Permission to enter, sir," Chief Kurikka said from the doorway.

"What? Chief—of course, come in. But why . . ."

He broke off when he saw that the chief was wearing his dress grays, the formal uniform of the spaceman. His hash marks were picked out in gold braid, and his high collar cut into his neck. Don realized he must have borrowed the grays from another spacer, since all of his own gear had been jettisoned. He came in, walking stiffly at attention—and behind him came the others.

They were all there, all in grays. Rama Kusum, engine room mate and sometime doctor. Purser Jonquet and Computerman Boyd. Sparks and the engineer, Tyblewski, and Air Tender Hansen. And behind them, in formal dress, head high and as stiff as the others, was Dr. Ugalde. He put his hand over his heart when they stopped and the others saluted.

"They couldn't all be here, the crew that is, Captain. But we represent them. And Dr. Ugalde, he's here because he is sure a part of the crew now."

"He certainly is that," Don said firmly, remembering what had happened, the course corrections and the matter of the counter-rebellion.

"We felt the same, sir. So he is here now when I, that is we, are here representing the crew. That is *your* crew, Captain."

Kurikka unbent from his stiff attention and looked down at Don. "I'm good at the proper ceremony, sir, when there *is* a proper ceremony, that is with the book and everything. Not that this isn't proper, it just isn't in the book. What I am trying to say is that the quarantine will be lifted in a few days and they want to take you to the hospital at Mars Central. Commander Doprava, there at the base, is going to con the Big Joe back to Earth orbit for repairs. But until he takes command you are still the captain." He snapped his fingers and a box was produced and handed to him.

"They can never take that away from you. Spacemen feel that there is nothing much higher than a captain of a ship. Not very many men make it. You did, sir, and you got us through and that is what counts." He opened the box and took out a peaked cap with a golden rocket on the front.

"This is a captain's hat. Yours now, because we bought it from the commander of the orbiter. It's from the crew, Captain. Every man chipped in."

Don took the cap in both hands, turning it around, and could find nothing to say. The men saluted. With emotion that he had never experienced before he returned the salute.

There were no words that could express how he felt, and they saw it on his face. This was their moment too, and they were united together by a tie that would never be broken. In silence, one by one, they left. Chief Kurikka was last and he hesitated in the doorway, then forced himself to speak.

"Captain, sir, could you tell me what you plan? I mean when you are out of the hospital. Most doctors serve a hitch in the space service, then practice dirtside. Nothing much to keep them in space, I guess. I wonder, your own plans, I mean . . ."

Don had planned to practice on one of the planets, there had never been any doubt about that. Yet, in that single instant, he realized what an impossible thing that would be to do. Dirtside—that was the only word for it. What did the globes of dust have to offer after the clear sharp world of space? There were deep-spacers to serve in, satellite research stations—endless opportunities once you thought about it. Yet, even as the thoughts were forming, he spoke.

"Don't believe any of that old scuttlebutt, Chief. I have no more intention of working dirtside than, well, than you do."

"Can't be more certain than that!" the chief said, smiling broadly. He snapped a salute and left.

The door closed and he was alone.

Don turned the cap over in his hands and ran his finger along the sleek gold cylinder of the emblem. Almost sorry that the voyage was ended. It was going to be a little tame, just being a doctor again.

"A rough voyage, and I'm glad it is over," he said softly to himself. "Very glad we are in a safe harbor at last. But I have this cap, and the memory of what it means. They can't ever take that away from me."